Taking the Town

By
Ford Murphy

Copyright 2016 by Ford Murphy
www. duncurra. com

Cover Design: Selectografix
Background image: Vincent Rafferty

ISBN-10:1-9426-2341-0
ISBN-13:978-1-9426-2341-0
Produced in the USA

Hey Old Friend!

Hope you
enjoy it.

Love

Ford !

Dedication

For My Family. Thank You.

Acknowledgements

Thanks to all those who helped make this book a reality.
Without your support, insight, constructive criticism and
guidance, it would have never have been possible. You
know who you are and I will always be very grateful.

Thanks also to Susan and all at Duncurra for taxing a chance
with an unknown, first time author. Your expert guidance has
been amazing and kept me from messing up a good story on
numerous occasions!

Thanks also to Vincent for the cover picture.
You did good, sir!

Prologue

Ten year old Finn Lane set out by himself to walk home. It was a four mile journey.He wasn't supposed to be alone and he knew he'd get into trouble for it.

He didn't care. He wanted to be alone.

He had traveled by bus with his soccer team to the north side of the city to play a game that would go a long way to determining who would become local champions for the year. Their opponents were an extremely tough team who had used a combination of skill and intimidation to remain unbeaten as of yet this season. They also had the advantage of near fanatical parental support lined up along the sidelines and shouting abuse at opposing players, often scaring them out of their wits.

Such tactics had worked particularly well in this game. So much so that Finn had become very angry with several of his team mates during the game because they were shirking tackles and not competing aggressively for the ball. Finn had thrown himself into every tackle with abandon and fought fiercely every time the ball came his way. They had been beaten by five goals to zero—their worst defeat of the season.

Finn was disgusted. He'd refused to ride the bus home with the team because he knew he would never be able to restrain himself. The walk would cool him off he thought. He wasn't entirely sure how to get home but he figured he knew enough to get him somewhere he recognized. He also knew he would be journeying alone through some pretty rough neighborhoods and he'd have to keep his wits about him the whole time.

He was still mentally running through the game as he walked home dejectedly, until he turned a corner and stopped short. Four boys, who had to be at least thirteen or fourteen, appeared to be picking on a girl who was maybe nine, at the most. They had surrounded her and were pushing her and pulling at her clothes. Even against those odds, Finn could see that she was not going down easily and was fighting back with all her might.

Finn ran towards them. "Leave her alone, you creeps! It's not right to pick on a little girl like that. What kind of boys are you?"

One of the teenagers looked at him. "Mind your own fecking business eejit." He turned back to the girl.

Finn shouted at them once more. "Stop it, I said. Leave her alone or you'll be sorry."

This had no effect either, so he switched tactics and shouted at the little girl. "Why don't you run away? They'll let you go."

When this latest entreaty invoked no response Finn decided if this little girl, who was completely outnumbered, was willing to fight back then he sure as hell could help her. He went flying in kicking and screaming like crazy. He started hitting at the boys and kept hitting.

"You want this you little shite? You got it." The older boys turned on him.

With their attention on him he shouted again at the little girl. "Run! Now—as fast as you can. Go home and call your dad and tell him I need help."

"No," she screeched back at him. "I'm not leaving. I can help."

"No you can't, girlie." One of the boys pushed her away. And she couldn't.

If the teens had been surprised by the ferocity and intensity of Finn's initial attack, it didn't last long. They ended up kicking the living shit out of him. They didn't stop until he was a bloody, bruised heap on the pavement. Then with one last kick, seemingly satisfied with the damage they had done, they walked away laughing and jostling each other, no longer interested in tormenting the little girl.

She rushed to him, tears pouring down her face. "Are you all right?"

"Yeah," he replied bravely, trying to hold back the tears that were welling up in his eyes. "Where do you live? I'll walk home with you to make sure they don't come back."

The little girl looked at him rather skeptically as if she was wondering how he thought he could protect her when he could barely stand up but she said, "Just around the corner."

Finn struggled to his feet. "Okay. Let's go."

It really was just around the corner. "There it is." She pointed.

He waited until she had the door open, then set off running.

"Hey wait," she shouted after him. "My parents will want to thank you."

He had already rounded the corner before she finished the sentence.

When Finn eventually arrived home, his parents' anger at his not traveling on the bus with his team quickly changed to concern when he told them what happened and they saw how badly bruised he was and how much pain he was in.

His mother inspected his face. "What were you thinking?" She lifted his shirt to check for broken ribs. "Why did you have to get involved?"

Finn looked at her for a moment, tears welling in his eyes. "How proud of me would you have been if I had stood and watched and let it happen? Would you have wanted me to walk away without helping?"

"Yes, I mean, no," his mother clucked. "I know you did the right thing but look at your poor face. My, my. You're such a brave little boy."

His father who had remained silent until now finally spoke up. "Well son, if you're going to stack the odds against yourself like that, we're going to have to get you some training in the art of fighting."

~ * ~

About two weeks later, the girl's parents found out where he lived and came to visit, bringing their daughter along.

Her father shook Finn's hand, appearing very somber. "Young man, I can't thank you enough."

Her mother hugged him. "You were so very brave. I can't even think about what would have happened if you hadn't intervened. She could have been...she could have been..." She seemed on the edge of tears. "Well, thank you."

The girl herself remained oddly silent during their visit. But as they were about to leave, she leaned over and kissed him on the cheek. "Thank you for saving me. Even though I didn't think I needed help at the time."

Finn blushed mightily and mumbled, "You're welcome." As she turned to leave he added, "I'd do it again you know."

And he knew he would. He also knew that if he couldn't stop something bad happening to her in the future, he'd make sure whoever did it paid dearly.

So, once his bruises cleared up, his father took him to a newly opened club where he was to learn how to fight.

The sport of mixed martial arts had been new to Ireland when Finn had started but he'd been hooked from the very first class. He loved the aggressive nature of the sport, the need for speed, reflexes, athletic ability, and above all, the requirement to keep a cool head and not panic in challenging situations. Fearlessness and a strong stomach for fighting were also huge advantages, both of which Finn had in abundance.

~ * ~

May, 1979
Eight Years Later

At eighteen there were no remnants of the scrawny kid Finn had once been. At six foot four he was two hundred and ten pounds of pure muscle and had developed into a genuine fighting machine. He was in Dublin for the All-Ireland Mixed Martial Arts Championship which was to be held over four days.

The sport had become very popular in Ireland and competition was expected to be intense for the top prizes. Finn was scheduled to compete in the heavyweight bracket and he knew he would be fighting against competitors in their late twenties and early thirties. He wasn't the least intimidated. He had trained hard for the past four months and his coaches believed he was ready.

But more importantly, Finn believed he was ready.

For several years his coaches had not only remarked on his abundance of ability and skill, they said he had *heart* and something else—something less definable. When he entered a ring, they said the look in his eyes became so intense it had an immediate effect on many of his opponents.

"One look from you makes many of your opponents want to be anywhere else in the world but standing opposite you in such a confined space."

His coaches expected him to do well. They thought that he might even go all the way, despite the high quality of the competition he was expected to face from older and far more experienced fighters.

As the competition progressed over four days, his coaches were proven right.

Finn had bulldozed his way through the earlier rounds, taking out his opponents with relative ease and without expending too much effort. He had surprised one of the tournament favorites in the semi-final with a blistering display of aggression and technique. Halfway through the second round his opponent had tapped out. Clearly the man knew if he didn't he was surely going to be knocked out.

A buzz had built up in the stadium about the teenage fighter from Cork who had easily taken apart the cream of the Irish MMA scene. By the time the final was held on the afternoon of the fourth day, the stadium was crammed with people eager to catch a glimpse.

"Completely jointed," his friend, David Kirk, had told Finn's parents when he phoned them about thirty minutes before the fight. "Not an empty seat in the house. Your boy is becoming a star. I'll get him to call you when the fight's over."

They didn't have to wait long for that call.

Finn knocked his opponent within fifteen seconds with a stunning kick that landed square on his jaw, lifting him off his feet before he fell prone on the canvas. There was stunned silence initially, as if nobody had ever seen anything like it. Then the whole stadium erupted in cheers.

His opponent was still out several minutes later when the referee held Finn's arm in the air and presented him with his belt. With that, Finn was crowned the first All-Ireland heavyweight MMA champion.

David rushed into the ring and hugged him fiercely. "Not bad for a gobshite from the 'Hane'," he shouted in glee, referring to the slang name for the parish where he and Finn had grown up.

His coaches smiled and exchanged high fives. Their protégé had announced his arrival on the big stage in the loudest possible manner.

Finn was to retain that crown for the next four years before bowing out of that competition undefeated to give others a chance at the title. Besides he was to set his sights higher on achieving international glory which most observers believed he had the ability to achieve.

Chapter One

Finn had recently completed a Ph.D. in his hometown of Cork and was eager and ready to make his mark on the world. He accepted the job at Roan Pharmaceuticals and relocated to Lissadown, a town of about twenty thousand located in the heart of the Irish midlands. Roan had been an unusual choice for him and he was not without misgivings. However, when he weighed everything thing up, he was convinced this was place to be…at least for now. He had a job to do.

He shared an office with Laura Jennings who held a Ph.D. in chemistry and had worked at Roan for several years. She was a friendly girl who was all of five feet tall with short brown hair and a pixie face. Finn had warmed to her immediately.

She looked up from her work and checked at her watch. "Wow, twelve thirty-four. Let's go to lunch. I'll introduce you to a few people. The food's not great but it's cheap and plentiful."

Finn shrugged. "Ok. Let's do it."

They left the small, somewhat dingy office in the low slung, redbrick building and walked out into the bright sunshine. Glancing down at her, Finn smiled to himself. They made for an interesting sight. The elfin Laura looked like a little kid next to Finn's broad shouldered, six foot four frame. Most people thought twice about getting on his wrong side and that suited Finn.

The canteen was located around the corner to the right of their building. It provided sustenance to the one hundred and fifty or so employees who were scattered across six small buildings. A much needed seventh building was under construction. Roan was doing very well and was widely recognized as a rising star in the pharmaceutical industry. It was also one of the very few indigenous Irish pharmaceuticals that conducted research on site, which was one of the reasons Finn wanted to come here.

They were all ugly buildings, some of them without windows and each with the same boring, red brick facade. The company was located on the outskirts of town surrounded on three sides by fields where cattle grazed. However, the cows were exponentially more pleasant neighbors than the pig factory on the fourth side. In truth it was not an inspiring location for this growing company but the land was cheap and the local officials had provided a lot of financial incentives to attract Roan to Lissadown.

Finn and Laura walked down steps into the canteen to be greeted by the hustle and bustle of the lunch time crowd and joined the line to purchase food. Finn looked at the food piled high in metal warming dishes. Laura was right, he thought. No one will ever accuse this establishment of serving haute cuisine.

As he waited in line, he surveyed the crowded room. Tables were jam packed with employees and he didn't miss the blatant stares of his new colleagues who appeared to study him intently. Unfazed, Finn shrugged it off. This was something he had become very used to. Men tended to look at him with a combination of envy and fear. On the other hand Finn knew women found him attractive. He worked hard to stay in peak condition but it was more than that. He'd had more than one woman tell him he gave off a "bad boy" vibe and they found that hint of danger to be very intriguing.

He continued to idly scan the room until his eyes came to rest on the person he sought. She sat at a table alone. There, for a brief moment, he looked directly into the green eyes he remembered so well, that were at once beautiful and sad. As lovely as her eyes were, he couldn't fail to notice how beautiful the rest of her was also. It seemed curious that she was dining all alone when pretty much every other table was full. He wondered if she was holding the table for her usual crew or if she was just early. As he held her gaze, the barest hint of red developed on her cheeks before she turned her eyes away.

Once they had picked their food up, he followed Laura to a table occupied by four women. Laura introduced him to each of them and he spent the next few minutes politely answering all of their questions about his background, his qualifications and why the hell he had come to Lissadown in the first place. Then the conversation moved on to "shop talk". Roan had recently obtained approval for one of its drugs and now it was all hands on deck to manufacture launch quantities. The production floor and quality control labs were operating twenty four hours a day, seven days a week. It was an exciting time for the company.

Still, despite all this Finn drifted in and out of the conversation as his attention kept straying to the table with the green-eyed beauty, the girl he'd come here for. All through lunch, she remained the sole occupant of the table even though most of the other tables eventually ended up virtually overflowing with occupants. He also noticed that nobody greeted her, spoke to her or even acknowledged her presence in any way. She just sat there alone and ate in silence, eyes down but with a certain pride and defiance in her demeanor.

He couldn't fathom why she was by herself. Eventually he couldn't hold his curiosity in anymore and asked, "What's with that table over there? Why is that girl all alone when every other table has more occupants than it was built for?"

His lunch companions went silent for a moment before someone replied, "It's not allowed. We can't sit with her."

Surely he hadn't heard right. "What do you mean it's not allowed? Not allowed by whom? Who gets to make that decision?" Finn looked at each one in turn.

When no response came, he tried again. "What? Is it a state secret or something?"

Laura whispered to him, "Not here. I'll tell you later when we're alone."

Finn could scarcely believe this. "Seriously?" Finn shook his head. "Okay. I can't wait to hear this."

Once they back to the office, Laura looked at him apologetically. "I'm sorry. I should have warned you about this in advance. It's just such a distressing story that I don't like to talk about it."

Finn frowned. "How bad can it be?"

"Very bad. But you need to know. So here goes." But she didn't say anything. She took a deep breath. "Okay, here goes," she repeated. "This is not a pleasant story and, to be honest, it's embarrassing—and it should be. Of everyone involved, the only person with any decency is the victim. The bad guys and those of us standing on the sidelines doing nothing, not so much."

She took another deep breath. This was clearly difficult for her.

"It may not look like it on the surface, Laura said, "but Lissadown is essentially under the control of a criminal gang comprised of three families who are all related to each other and who live close to each other in a virtual no-go compound. They and their henchmen rule the roost over Lissadown with a virtual iron fist and are allowed to operate unimpeded and untouched by the law. These criminals have made life so miserable for many people the past few years. They have blackmailed businesses, they control the drug trade and have even been responsible for several murders, not to mention the disappearance of at least four people who dared to stand up to them. That girl at the table in the canteen, Julia Davis, had a brother, Brian.

He is one of those gone missing."

Finn said nothing. He just sat there and listened with his eyes never once straying from Laura's face. He knew part of the story—it's why he came to Lissadown—but he needed the details.

Laura sighed heavily and continued her story. "Brian Davis intervened when gang members started to beat up a friend of his over the late payment of a debt. Ordinarily, Brian would have received a severe beating himself for this intervention and that would have been the end of it. Apparently, however, one of the gang members had pulled a knife on him and as they and he had wrestled for it, the gang member ended up getting stabbed with his own knife—apparently because of his own clumsiness. Brian didn't have anything to do with it but that didn't satisfy the gang member and his crew who then became hell bent on revenge. A week later, Brian Davis went missing. That was almost eighteen months ago, in fact just a few weeks after Julia herself had arrived in Lissadown. There has been no sign of him since."

Laura sat back in her chair and wiped a tear from her eye then blew her nose before continuing. "Julia became frantic after he had been missing for two days. She knew what happened with the gang member and she feared the worst for her brother. She initially pestered the police to try to find out what had happened to him but to be honest they were too afraid to intervene. The cops in this town also have family members who have been targeted by the gang and in fact several of them have moved relatives out of the country for protection." Her tone was almost apologetic.

So that explained the distinct lack of police involvement.

"Days turned into weeks and still no sign of Brian, and then weeks into months. As time passed, Julia became even more determined in her efforts to find out what happened and where her brother was. All by herself, she would confront every gang member she could find and get right in their faces." Laura shook her head. "I tell you, Finn, this girl has courage. She even went as far as to stand outside their houses with a placard calling them murderers and demanding justice. People tried to get her to stop but it seemed the more they tried the more aggressive her tactics became. As I said she is one brave lady.

This didn't surprise him at all. Julia would jump in with both fists flying.

"Lots of men have just put their heads down and not engaged with these thugs in any way but not Julia. She was like a force of nature. She even took to following the gang leaders in the street and calling them cowards and low life scum. Really crazy stuff. It's almost like she was daring them to react. Well of course they did. One night she was grabbed just as she was about to enter her front door. Apparently, there were six of them and they drove her out to the bog where they all raped her…repeatedly." Laura's voice trailed off and she looked away, remaining silent for a moment.

This was much worse than he expected and it turned his stomach. But he had to hear it all. "What happened then?" Finn prodded.

"By the time they were finished she was almost dead. They just left her there…in the bog…alone." Laura swiped at another errant tear. "Most people figure they thought she was dead or soon would be. They aren't known for leaving living victims. But the funny thing is, against all odds, Julia somehow managed to make her way to the nearest house— almost two miles away. The people who found her said it looked as if she had crawled most of the way. But she did it. She remained conscious until the ambulance arrived. Then she was out of it for days. For the first three days it was touch and go as to whether she would survive and, if she did, what condition she would be in. To the doctors' immense surprise—they had written her off by then—she began to pull though. I've heard people say that no one believed she'd ever fully recover. It was miraculous that she survived at all. But incredibly, after six weeks Julia was well enough to return to work."

Laura stopped talking and looked at Finn. "Do you want to hear more or has it all been too sordid for you?"

He didn't want to hear another word. He didn't want to imagine the horror of it. But he had to know. "It hasn't been easy to hear all of this, but I need to know how it ends."

Laura nodded and continued. "Even after all that, those bastards couldn't let her be. It's not like she hadn't suffered enough by then. Her brother was missing, presumably dead, and she herself had been raped and beaten almost to her own death. No, that wasn't enough. So when Julia came back to work, the gang put the word out—no one at Roan was to have anything to do with her. Other than what is required for work, no one was allowed to talk to her, sit with her, eat with her or travel to and from work with her. I'm not sure if you know but there are six known gang members working at Roan and they keep everyone else in line. No one is willing to stand up to them and disobey their orders. That only compounds the tragedy. As I said, the only decent people in this whole story are the victims. The rest of us, myself included, we should be ashamed of ourselves for our cowardice. There are times when I hate myself over this."

"But didn't the police do anything at all? Surely they'd have to act on such a vicious crime."

Laura shook her head. "No, they didn't. Just like the rest of us cowards, they just buried their heads in the sand and got on with their own lives. This whole town is such a shit-hole for allowing this to happen and continuing to let it go on every day."

"Just when did all this occur?" Finn asked.

Laura responded, "I think Julia has now been back at

work for about eight months."

Finn was incredulous. "You mean to say that for the last eight months, not one person in this company has spoken to her at all?"

Laura's face burned with intense shame. "Yes. What they did...it fucking worked. It put the town on warning. Effectively saying, *this is what happens when you cross us.* Everyone is terrified. I know I am."

Finn frowned. "But this can't be allowed to go on."

She stared intently at him, the tone of her voice deadly serious. "I'm telling you, you have no idea what these people are like. They're complete animals. If you want my advice, as pathetic as it is, stay away from them. Don't interfere. Don't even let them know you exist and you'll survive. It's what we all do." She shook her head, disgustedly. "God, I've got to get out of here." With that she practically ran out of the office leaving Finn sitting there contemplating the enormity of the story she had just told him. It was exponentially worse than he'd expected.

That night as he worked out, his head was full of thoughts of Julia Davis and her beautiful green eyes. His fury began to build thinking of the savages who had taken Brian and who had brought her to the brink of her own death. The fact that they held the entire town in their evil grip was unexpected news that only fueled the fire in him. As his fists crashed into the punching bag, his mind became set.

Chapter Two

Tuesday, June 24, 1986
Week One: Day Two

Finn was up early that morning after a fitful night. At five-thirty he went for a ten mile run with his heavily weighted back pack tight against his shoulders. He followed this up with a punishing weights and abs session before arriving to work at eight-thirty.

The morning drifted by in a series of meetings until lunch time arrived. Once again, he and Laura headed for the canteen.

As they looked at the selections, he wrinkled his nose. "Starting next week, I'm going to pack my own lunch. I'm just a little afraid of the long term consequences of a daily dose of this swill."

When he'd selected the lesser of several evils, he started to follow Laura to where they'd eaten yesterday. But just before he got there, he turned suddenly and walked directly to the table that was occupied by the solitary figure of Julia Davis.

"Hi, I'm Finn." He stuck out his hand. "Finn Lane. I'm new. Yesterday was my first day."

Julia just stared, first at his outstretched hand then into his eyes as a look of sheer terror spread across her face. She glanced around nervously before quietly saying, "You can't sit here." When he made no move to leave, she added, "It's not allowed."

Meanwhile, a deathly silence had engulfed the entire room and all eyes were trained on their table.

"Please," she pleaded almost in a whisper but with a palpable urgency. "Please leave now. It's not safe."

Finn looked at her steadily. "What's not safe? The food? You?"

"Just go, please before it's too late. They're watching," Julia begged.

"I just want to sit and have lunch with you." He flashed her a grin. "Come on, is that such an unpleasant prospect for you? I promise, I do have reasonably acceptable table manners."

Before she could answer, he heard people in the room gasp and felt a presence behind him.

"You can't sit at that table."

Finn turned around. Three men stood there, staring menacingly.

Finn kept his tone casual. "I don't understand. There's plenty room at this table and this girl was all alone so I thought I'd sit with her. What's wrong with that?"

"You're not allowed to sit there. It's the rule. *Nobody* sits at the table with *her*." The man leaned closer, clearly attempting to intimidate Finn. The other two continued to stare at him with murderous looks in their eyes.

Finn held their gaze for a few seconds then shrugged and in a quiet voice said, "I'm sorry. I'm new. I didn't know. It won't happen again."

"It had better not. See that it doesn't."

As the trio walked walked out of the canteen, the room seemed to heave a collective sigh of relief and conversation began again, quietly at first then gradually increasing in volume.

Finn turned back to Julia and took the seat opposite her. "Nice guys those three. I think I like them."

Julia's green eyes flashed angrily at him. "Do you think this is funny? I can tell you it's not. Are you trying to be a hero or are you just completely fucking stupid? This is not a game."

"Whoa." Finn put up a hand. "Steady. I didn't mean to upset you. I shouldn't have made light of the situation. Can we start over?" He glanced around. "They're gone. I guess we get to have lunch after all now."

She glared at him for a few more seconds then heaved a sigh. "I'm Julia Davis but I guess you know that already. And I'm sure you've heard by now the details of my sordid story. So Dr. Finn Lane from Cork with the death wish, I'm all ears. Tell me your story."

"Ignoring the whole death wish thing, how did you know I'm *Dr.* Finn Lane *from Cork*?"

"I saw the notice on the new hire board announcing that you'd been hired. But aside from that, there are no secrets around Roan."

They chatted as they ate and he was more and more drawn to her. Their lunch break was nearly over, but he wanted more time with her. "Hey, what do you do at night? Do you go to the pub, the movies or go for walks? What?"

Her eyes clouded over. "I sit at home alone most nights. Sometimes, I go for long drives, find somewhere to park, then walk awhile. Not often though because it's dangerous trying to get back into my house at night and…"

"And what? Bad memories?"

Julia nodded. "Horrific memories. Whatever you heard, trust me it was far, far worse than anyone can imagine."

"I could drop by and keep you company sometime." Finn smiled. "I could do with a friend in this God forsaken town also."

"Thanks." She shook her head. "But that would not be a good idea." She glanced at her watch. "Look, I've got to get back to work." She stood and started to walk away, but stopped after a few steps and turned around. "It was nice having someone to talk to. I appreciate it, but don't do it again."

When he got back to the office, that warning was echoed by a steady stream of people who dropped by to tell him how dangerous a stunt he had pulled and that he was now a marked man.

His boss and his boss's boss each summoned him separately to their offices to deliver the same message. "This is very serious. People have disappeared and have died. Do not cross these thugs. You will suffer badly if you do."

After Finn assured everyone that it was a once off event, he spent the rest of the afternoon trying to concentrate on his work. He found he couldn't though as his mind was drawn time and time again to those vivid green eyes, the black curly hair and the perfectly formed mouth of Julia Davis' beautiful face. *Shit. I'm falling for her. That was fast.*

That night after he had completed another workout session, he walked through town. Although it was almost ten o'clock, it was still light and the breeze was warm. Everyone he met seemed to keep their heads down, avoiding eye contact as they walked hurriedly by him.

This is such a sad place...so little joy...so much unhappiness.

He continued his stroll and found himself wandering down the street where he knew Julia lived. There was no question as to which house was hers. It was easily identifiable by the graffiti scrawled all over the walls and door. The words *whore, cunt* and *assfuck*, featured prominently along with drawings of men doing all sorts of nasty things to a woman he supposed was meant to depict Julia.

"Poor girl." Finn sighed. "She's suffered enough."

As he continued walking down the street, a group of four young men approached, stopping in front of him. "Looking for something?" one of the little shits asked.

Finn shook his head. "No. Just out for a stroll on this fine night. I assume you boys don't have a problem with that. Right?" He looked from one set of eyes to the next. Although his tone of voice was mild, he made certain the look he gave each of them said, "Don't mess with me. You won't like the outcome."

"You looking for trouble, you fucking prick?" asked another one, "because you found it."

"Have I?" Finn stared hard at him for a moment. His eyes narrowed, but his tone was mild. "Your move. I'm waiting."

And wait he did. He simply stood there, totally

relaxed until the four thugs seemed to realize they were outgunned, lost their nerve and walked away.

"Next time, motherfucker. You'll get yours," shouted one after they were a safe distance away."

Finn chuckled softly. *Not from you, you little asswipe*. As he began to walk away, he turned his head and caught a brief movement in an upstairs window of Julia's house.

"You see," he said to the now empty window. "There is no need to live in constant fear. Consider this a small, first step. Now you sleep well. I don't think they'll bother you anymore tonight."

Finn walked home in the dark with a smile on his face. *Who knows? I might get to like it here after all*.

~ * ~

Later, Julia Davis sat alone in her living room nursing a glass of wine. For a while, after she had recovered from the attack, she had wanted to leave Lissadown, but the gang blocked every attempt. Her savings were tied up in the house so she tried to put it on the market. Oddly, no estate agent would take it. She made an attempt at selling it herself. A few people came to see it who initially seemed interested but every one of them backed out.

At the same time she put her house up for sale, she began searching for another job. But either jobs were not easy to come by or the gang's reach was farther than she imagined because she received no response to her inquiry letters.

Without being able to sell her house or find another job, there wasn't anywhere else for her to go. Both of her parents were dead and she had no other sibling besides Brian. With him gone too, she was all alone.

Barred at every turn, she figured the gang wanted her to stand as a living warning to anyone else who considered crossing them. Eventually she had reached the point where she no longer cared whether she lived or died herself.

Somehow that was what galvanized her determination to stay. Her life was empty. She didn't have anyone and she knew she was never going to meet someone now, not after what those animals had done to her. The very thought of a man touching her or being intimate made her skin crawl. But she was alive and she was not going to let them take her home or her job or anything else from her.

Despite all of her strength and resolve, lately she was beginning to find her determination to stay in Lissadown was beginning to wane. Her constant loneliness and isolation, coupled with the ongoing harassment she faced almost daily, had brought her to the brink of leaving and seeking a fresh start even if it meant waiting tables and living from hand to mouth. Lunch today was the first time in a long while that she had interacted socially with someone from Roan and that was with a new guy who apparently didn't seem to know any better.

Still, she had found Finn quite intriguing. He did not seem at all intimidated when he was confronted in the canteen and she felt sure he knew how to handle himself which, she thought, was a very useful skill to have these days in Lissadown.

Although Julia had stopped looking at men in that way after her attack, she had to admit that Finn was extremely good looking. There was something about him that could suck a person in. Strong but kind. The type of guy a woman knew she'd be safe with. This was something decidedly lacking in Julia's life at the moment.

"Ah, bullshit," she exclaimed bitterly to the empty room. "As if he'd even be remotely interested in me anyway. He was just being polite. Don't fool yourself."

Julia was so ashamed of how her body looked after the attack. She did everything she could not to see herself naked and she knew for certain that she was never going to let a man see her body again.

She sipped her wine pensively in the dark. She heard someone outside yell something that ended in *motherfucker*, but hearing obscenities hurled her direction was nothing new. She ignored it.

Yes, she needed to bite the bullet and just leave. Then Finn's face came into her mind again, causing a small smile to form on her lips. "Maybe I'll give it a few more days before I tell them I'm leaving. What difference could a few more days make in the grand scheme of things?"

Chapter Three

June, 1983
Three Years Earlier
University College, Cork

One morning when Finn arrived at his laboratory in UCC to work on his experiments, he found a note on his desk from his professor requesting a meeting in his office as soon as possible. It was the beginning of Finn's third year as a chemistry post-grad and his progress towards his doctorate was in good shape so he knew he wasn't in any trouble. He was a dedicated student. While he did attend a few of the many parties that were a feature of post-grad life, he rarely drank a lot and he certainly stayed away from the drugs that circulated freely at these events. Finn was very focused on his training and anything that interfered with his progress in MMA was to be avoided.

Lately, he had expressed his frustration with the lack of modern equipment and technology to his professor but he wasn't alone in that. It was a pretty common complaint among post-grads. Still, he was curious about what the boss could want so he headed out of the lab to his professor's office on the third floor.

Finn knocked on the door.

"Enter," the professor called tersely. His bark was far worse than his bite and his outwardly gruff demeanor hid an excellent academic who took a real interest in his students.

Finn opened the door. Professor Trevor Hathaway's office was compact and rudimentary and held a distinct aroma of the many chemicals that occupied the shelves on the wall next to his many books and publications. Finn often doubted that this was an entirely safe set-up but he kept his mouth shut. "You wanted to see me, boss?"

"Yes, I did, Finn." The older man motioned for him to sit down then glared at him for a moment. "So, you've been unhappy with the quality of the equipment here. Holding back your research are we? Not able to make as much as progress as a brilliant scientist such as yourself should be able to, eh?"

Finn looked at him apologetically. "I'm sorry. I was just blowing off steam. Don't take any notice of that. You know I didn't mean it."

"Well, as a matter of fact," a broad smile spread across Professor Hathaway's face, "I happen to agree with you. And, I happened to have done something about it."

Finn looked at him quizzically. "Are we getting—"

The professor cut him off with a wave of his hand. "No, to answer the question you were about to ask, we are not getting new equipment. No money in the budget for that. Instead, I'm sending Mohammed to the mountain."

Finn was totally lost. "I'm sorry, sir. I don't understand."

"Ah, you see, Finn, you think I'm just some old fogey prof operating here in obscurity, don't you?"

He grinned. "Actually, that part might be true but I do have some contacts with the outside world."

"Honestly, boss, I'm completely stumped about where this is going."

Hathaway frowned. "Right. I do have a tendency to take the long route to my point, don't I?"

Finn smiled and shrugged. "Your words, not mine."

The professor laughed. "Okay, to the point. You, my friend, have an opportunity to spend six months in the very modern laboratory of Professor Richard Spalding in KenTech in America. I've collaborated with him on a number of projects that have led to well received publications. I mentioned to him that you were somewhat unhappy with the lack of resources here and he made the offer. His lab is as modern as they come and his research is in an adjacent field to ours so he'll be able to help and guide you." He beamed at Finn. "So, what do you think? Will you go?"

Finn simply sat there with his mouth open for a moment. "I...well...I...wow," was all he could manage at first. Then he leapt up from his chair, wrapped his professor in a bear hug and shouted, "Yes. Thank you so much. Yes, yes, yes."

"Great. I was hoping that would be your response, though I hadn't factored in having my ribs crushed in the process."

Finn shrugged, feeling the color rise in his cheeks. "Sorry," he muttered apologetically, "I got carried away."

Hathaway laughed. "That's fine. They'll heal

eventually. Now as for logistics. You'll need a visa and you also need to finish and write up a couple of key experiments here before you go. But more importantly, you need to be here to help the chemistry department win the Quarry Cup for the first time ever. I'm liable to be shot if I send you to America during the competition, particularly when this is our best chance in years of winning the cup in living memory. All in all, I'd say you should plan on leaving in four weeks."

Finn smiled at Hathaway. The Quarry Cup was a bi-annual soccer competition between all of the different departments in the university. It was fiercely competitive and the games were no place for the faint of heart. Typically, one of the engineering faculties won out in the end. Though there had been occasions when the Agricultural Science department, or the *Cowpunchers* as they were more commonly known, put together a winning team.

The Chemistry department had a dismal record and were usually eliminated from the competition without a whimper at the earliest stage possible. This year, however, they had won their first three games and were progressing nicely. They had somehow amassed a combination of skilled players who could score goals as well as those who could prevent the opposition from scoring.

Finn fell squarely into the latter classification. He was a bulwark on the team and his size, speed and commitment to the tackle more than compensated for his lack of finesse. He had been a reasonable player in his younger days and enjoyed the game but he was under no illusion whatsoever why he was so important to the team. Put simply, opponents were afraid of him. This was proving to be a big advantage in the Chemistry department's quest to win the Quarry Cup for the very first time.

"Four weeks it is," he said to Hathaway. "I'll get all my work completed by then. I can't make any guarantees about the Quarry Cup but I'll certainly be out there swinging. I can't thank you enough for this." Finn started to leave the office, but turned back around. "By the way, where the hell is KenTech?"

Hathaway grinned. "I wondered when you were going to ask that. 'KenTech' is what most people call the The Kentucky Institute of Technology. It's a university of about eight thousand students located in the town of Edgarville, in Eastern Kentucky."

"Eastern Kentucky? That sounds like the middle of nowhere."

"Don't be fooled. It is a small town—roughly forty thousand people—and it's about a two hour drive from Frankfort, the state capitol. But KenTech is a science and engineering college with an excellent reputation for the quality of its academic standards. It is also remarkably well-funded and its students and professors enjoy resources that are well beyond the reach of UCC and, indeed, most universities."

"Have you ever been there?"

The old professor chuckled. "Yes, Finn, I have. I think you will find it friendly and picturesque—a typical southern town. However, with students and academics from all over the country, it also tends to be remarkably progressive in many ways.

Finn grinned. "I can't wait. And I can't thank you enough. Considering the critical juncture I'm at in my research, having this opportunity is unbelievable."

~ * ~

His parents were delighted when he told them and his friends were jealous.

"How come you get to go?" one of them asked as they were sitting in the bar.

"Because, my friend," Finn replied, "I'm responsible and reliable and I won't do anything to damage the college's reputation. You on the other hand..." He canted his head to one side. "Need I say more?"

"Point taken," his friend replied. "I wouldn't send me either—not when I have the option of sending the Virgin Mary herself."

Finn laughed. He was used to this good natured ribbing and he knew his friends were actually excited for him. Once they knew he'd be around to see out the Quarry Cup, they were willing to forgive anything.

"I do have one favor to ask though," Finn said. "I need to run an experiment in the isolation lab on the sixth floor and I need someone with me at all times. So I'm looking for volunteers to stay with me in shifts."

"What's the experiment?" one of them asked.

"Yes, well, there's the catch. For one of the steps I need to make cyanide gas—enough to knock off the whole department, if it escapes. I'll understand, if you guys want to wuss out and leave me there all by myself."

One of them threw a beer mat at Finn. "Of course we're going to wuss out. Then when you don't make it down from the sixth floor, we're going to fight over who goes to America in your place."

Finn laughed. "Good to know I have the support and love of my friends."

Brid, one of the girls in his lab, asked, "When are you starting?"

"Tomorrow."

"Okay, I'll take first shift."

"I'll take second shift," said Ann, followed by Eileen who said she'd do third shift.

"You rotten son of a bitch," said his friend Frank. "Now you get to be alone in the isolation lab with half the girls in the department. I should hate you."

Finn laughed. "I guess you're up for fourth shift, so?"

He sat back and smiled. These were such good people. He was definitely going to miss them.

Chapter Four

Wednesday, June 25, 1986
Week One: Day Three

Finn woke up early as usual and worked out hard. At age twenty five, he knew he was entering his prime. His body felt strong and responsive as he tested its limits. Following a light breakfast he settled in his office by eight to start the day's work.

Shortly afterwards a guy he didn't recognize peered around the door and said, "Hey, there's a rumor going around that you like to work out. Some of the guys saw you in the gym the other night. A bunch of us work out most lunch times at a gym in town and we were wondering if you'd like to come along. It's all very casual so suit yourself."

All very casual. Right. Finn smiled. "Well, I'm only starting to train so I'm not sure I'd be up to your standards but thanks anyway."

"Sure," the guy said looking directly at Finn with a hint of a challenge in his eyes and in his voice. "I understand if you're concerned or nervous but this is all very friendly and non-combative. Honestly, you'll be fine so please come along."

Finn considered him for a moment. The last sentence was definitely a challenge and no way was he going to back down. "Okay. Thanks. But you guys will have to be patient with me. Where do I go?"

The guy in the doorway positively beamed and

gave Finn the address before he left with a big smile plastered across his face.

Finn watched him leave. "Hmm. Laura, I'll warrant there's more to that than meets the eye."

"You think?" she replied sarcastically. "It's a complete set up. That's where they hang out. The gang, that is. There's no way you can go. Seriously, tell me you're joking."

Finn shook his head. "I'm going. I want to see what their next move is."

Laura spluttered, "Are you fucking serious? What do you think their next move will be? They're going to beat the fucking shit out of you. Do you have some kind of death wish or something? Because you are so playing with fire."

Finn smiled at her. "It's fine. Trust me. It will all work out."

At a little after one, Finn walked into a dank and dreary gym. There were about twenty five guys there, all decked out in shorts and tee-shirts, all heavily muscled and some covered in tattoos.

The guy from Roan saw him and came over. "Glad you could make it. Welcome. After you warm up why don't you spar with one of the guys. It will help you settle in."

"Thanks," Finn said and set about his stretching routine.

After about fifteen minutes he said he was ready and climbed into the ring. He wasn't a bit surprised when three others followed him.

"So, maggot," one of them said, "you think you're a tough guy? Well let's see how tough you are." With that they spread out around the ring and adopted fighting positions.

Finn wasn't worried. He could already tell they had strength and basic technique but no craft. Before stepping through the door, he'd decided how to play this. Showing his cards too early would not be beneficial in the long run. He intended to take the middle ground, demonstrate enough to make them think but not so much that they became truly suspicious. That meant he'd have to take few hits.

When the session was over, Finn was still standing but sported multiple bruises to his face and other parts of his body. His antagonists high fived each other and sneered at him.

"Remember this lesson, maggot. We let you off easily. Next time you won't be so fucking lucky."

Finn just nodded his head and left. A satisfied smile split his face when he was outside. The eejits bought it.

Laura clucked over him when he returned to the office. "I told you so. Actually, I think you got away lightly."

"That's what they said too. I don't want to talk about it anymore. I have work to do."

Later that afternoon, the story spread through town that a thirteen-year-old girl had been blinded and her fifteen-year-old brother had his tongue cut out because their father had provoked a senior gang member by refusing to pay protection money for his little grocery store. The father had himself been beaten up several times but now the gang had turned on his kids in order to send him and everyone else a message about the consequences of not following orders.

When Finn first heard the news, he was outraged. Sadistic bastards. *What kind of monsters would do that to young kids?* He shook his head. He knew the answer. *The same kind that would do what they did to Julia Davis.* There should be no place in the world for that sort. They deserved a taste of their own medicine. *I won't forget this.*

Finn was amazed that there was no public outrage, no statement from the police about the action they were taking, no apparent reaction other than a further tightening of the noose around this beleaguered town. *What's wrong with this place? How can a whole town lose its nerve and sense of dignity? These people must truly live in abject terror.*

~ * ~

Later that night, Julia was startled by a knock at her door. After first peeking through the window to see who it was, she cautiously opened the door to Finn Lane.

"Fuck them. This is not right. I won't stand for it. You mark my words." He stormed away and left her standing staring at his back.

"Wow," Julia said aloud when she went back inside. "Wow, wow, wow. This guy is really something." He was already the talk of Roan and possibly even the whole town by now. "You have certainly stirred the hornet's nest, Dr. Finn Lane from Cork. Yes, indeed."

She thought about him for a moment. In another life, she would have wanted to get to know him and would have loved to spend time with him. But this wasn't another life. This was her shitty life in Lissadown. Outcast, rape victim, burned and scarred. There was no future in having such thoughts about Finn Lane. She didn't need any more hurt.

Chapter Five

February, 1986
Four Months Earlier
West Cork

On a bright, crisp Friday afternoon, Finn left college early and got in his car to make the long drive out to West Cork to spend the weekend with his friend, David Kirk, and David's family. He and David had been best buddies since primary school and had remained very close after David, his mother and sister moved out of the city, to their summer home in West Cork shortly after Mr. Kirk had tragically passed away after a massive heart attack.

Finn and David had grown up together in those inner-city mean streets and had learned how to take care of themselves and their families. Shortly after Finn's father took him to join the new mixed martial arts club in Cork, David joined too. Together they progressed through the ranks to become experts in street fighting and garnering the calm confidence that young men have when they know nobody is going to mess with them.

He missed David a lot and thought they didn't see enough of each other so he was delighted when David rang him and asked him to come down to celebrate his sister, Margo's, twenty second birthday.

"I can't believe she's twenty-two already," Finn mumbled to himself, "and so much trouble to boot."

Margo had had a serious crush on Finn for years and threw herself at him every time they saw each other. He knew this time would be no different and after a few drinks he would have to be very careful.

After driving almost four hours, Finn finally pulled into the long driveway that led to a large, open plan house overlooking Roaring Water Bay. David now worked at a multinational computer company that had established operations twenty miles away while Margo was getting ready to begin teaching next year at the local primary school.

As he parked, the door to the house opened and Margo came running out. "Finn Lane, you get more sexy every time I see you! Get over here and give the birthday girl a hug and a kiss."

She wrapped her arms around his neck, pulled him tightly towards her and kissed him firmly on the lips. As usual, her kiss was a couple of seconds longer and more intense than a regular kiss between friends. He could feel the swell of her breasts against his chest and the slow, rhythmic grind of her crotch against his. Her bright blue eyes sparkled devilishly as she gazed intensely at him. He could also feel the unbidden stirrings of his body.

So did Margo. She pressed herself even closer against him. "Take me away and make me a woman," she murmured in a husky tone as she nibbled his earlobe.

As he struggled to untangle himself from her grasp before it became too late to retain his composure, he heard a voice say, "Margo Kirk, kindly unhand that boy this instant! There'll be no woman making in my house this weekend."

Margo stepped back. "Sorry mom," she said with complete insincerity. Then she mouthed *later* to Finn as she walked away.

"That child," grumbled David's mother. "It's worse she's getting."

"Hi Mrs. K. It's great to see you, and thank you."

"You're welcome. How are your parents?"

"Great. They were asking for you."

"Well, I miss them terribly. David should be home shortly. Come on in. I know you could probably murder a beer, right?"

"Is the bear a Catholic?" Finn responded using the old mixed metaphor joke that he and David had "invented" many years ago. *It's good to be here.* This was one place he could just be himself.

When David got home, before dinner, he and Finn went for a walk on the cliffs right along the shoreline to catch up on all the gossip. David looked good. He was working out just as much as Finn even though he was now employed full time. They compared notes on training techniques, complained about the sports teams they supported and worked on their plans for a trip to Africa they intended to make next year. This had been a dream of theirs for years and now, with David working and Finn close to finishing up in college, it was starting to become a reality.

"Margo will kill both of us if we go without her," David warned.

"I know. But I think I'd rather risk her wrath

than spend a whole month keeping her out of my bed."

David laughed. "Good luck this weekend, buddy. She's on a mission."

Margo Kirk was not classically pretty but she was very sexual and she knew she had a great body. She was also shameless at exposing it to Finn. Once a couple of years ago, when both of them were sunbathing on the isolated cliffs overlooking the harbor and David had gone back to the house, she stripped off her bikini top and lay there with her breasts exposed, reveling in Finn's discomfort.

"Do I have nice tits?" she'd asked. "Better than others you've seen?"

"I'm not answering that, and put your top on."

"Why? I'm just trying to get an even tan all over."

Finn shook his head and looked away.

"Okay, I'll put my top on if you come over here and suck my nipple. Otherwise, I'm taking my bottom off too and I got my pussy waxed just for you. I'm all hairless and smooth as a baby's bum."

"Well," Finn said as he stood up, "I'm sure the people coming over the cliff will appreciate the view." Then he set off running back to the house.

"Wimp," he heard her call as he put distance between them.

He would need some luck this weekend. He didn't want to insult or hurt her but she was like a sister. *Even if I wanted to it's never going to happen.*

In truth, Margo unnerved him a little. She had always seemed a little unbalanced to him and he knew that she had a really mean streak in her. She was not the type to forgive or forget anyone who did anything or upset her in any way.

Besides, he'd given his heart away years ago. It was complicated but he couldn't find a way out of it.

They arrived back at the house just as Mrs. Kirk was getting ready to serve dinner.

"Oh look, it's the lovebirds," giggled Margo. "All pink cheeked and cheery after their lovers stroll."

"Margo," her mother scolded, "stop."

"Oh come on, Mom, they love it. Don't you, boys?"

"So this looks great, Mrs. K," Finn said, changing the subject. "Thanks again for having me."

"You should thank me." Margo pouted. "After all, it's my birthday and my idea. No wait." She laughed coyly. "You can thank me later."

And so it went all through dinner, lots of banter, teasing and more than enough direct come-ons from Margo.

"Have any news on the job front, Finn?" David's mother asked when they had left the table and were sitting comfortably in the sun room.

"As a matter of fact I do. It looks like I'll be joining Roan Pharmaceuticals in Lissadown in a few months, once I get my thesis wrapped up."

"What? Where?" David looked astonished. "You never told me that."

"It's not one hundred percent certain yet, so I was keeping it to myself until I knew for sure but, hey, I can trust you guys."

"Why the fuck would you want to go to Lissadown to work for some fucking no name company? Are you out of your fucking mind?" David spluttered.

"David," Margo admonished in a mock stern voice, "that's not fair. Just because he is out of his fucking mind doesn't mean you have to rub his nose in it. It's difficult enough for him without that."

"Thanks, you guys." Finn smiled. "I knew I could count on your understanding and support."

Mrs. Kirk, who had stayed silent during that exchange, now said, "Roan Pharmaceuticals? Don't we know someone there?"

"I don't think so, Mrs. K," Finn replied.

"No, I'm pretty sure we do. It will come to me."

"Just like Finn to me," Margo said and roared with laughter at her own joke. "Hey by the way, what was the name of that little girl you saved from those four teenagers when you were ten or eleven?"

"That was a pretty random question, Margo," David said. "Why'd you bring her up?"

Margo shrugged. "I don't know. What was her name, Finn?"

"Ah Jesus, I can't remember her name," Finn said. "It was almost fifteen years ago."

"What do you mean?" Margo asked. "You're still in touch with her, right?"

"No, I'm not," Finn responded indignantly. "Definitely not."

Margo laughed. "Whoa, buddy. Me thinketh the boy protesteth too much. I heard a rumor that she was having difficulties with a guy a few years ago. Then suddenly, out of the blue somebody shows up and hey presto, no more problem. Has your finger prints all over it."

"You're wrong. I haven't seen her in over ten years."

"No one said you had to have seen her. You could have just swooped in like Batman with his cape and cleaned up the situation."

"Are you jealous, Mags?" David asked.

"Damn straight I am. I'm not standing for acne headed, scrawny bitch with fried egg tits having a hold over my man."

"She doesn't…" Finn started but thought better.

"She doesn't what, Finn?" Margo asked. "Have acne? Fried egg tits? Or a hold over *my man*?" Margo laughed. "Look at him, he's blushing. You are in contact with her."

"I'm not. Honest."

"That's enough out of you, Margo Kirk," said her mother. "Finn, I would love a visit from your parents. Let them know they are welcome at any time."

Luckily, the conversation moved on from there, but he could see Margo looking at him quizzically throughout the evening.

He got on the road back to Cork on Sunday afternoon after a wonderful weekend. He and David were all caught up and he had successfully kept Margo out of his bed. *A good result all round.* He grinned as he turned on the radio.

Chapter Six

Thursday, June 26, 1986
Week One: Day Four

As soon as Finn opened his eyes that morning he knew today was a pivotal day. If conflict was going to come it would be as a result of his actions today. He knew he could still take the easy road. He could defuse the situation entirely and he was pretty sure that there would be no additional fall out. On the other hand, he could raise the stakes, turn up the heat and set the train in motion.

"Hah," he said derisively. "Like I have a frigging choice either way."

Even so he had to walk a fine line. He didn't want the showdown to come today. He just wanted to finish laying the groundwork. He needed to ensure that the conflict would go from zero to sixty, on his terms, with no room for any moderation.

Yes, today is a big day indeed.

He decided to forego his usual morning workout and after a shower and a light breakfast, he set off on the roughly two mile walk out of town to Roan. It was a bright summer morning and the walk felt good. Since it was early there was very little traffic on the road, making it a peaceful journey for him. He clocked in early, grabbed a cup of coffee from the little kitchen near his office and settled in to read some research reports. After a while, he could hear people start to drift in and the peace and quiet that he had been enjoying evaporated.

Laura arrived at eight twenty-five and the very first words out of her mouth were, "Hey Finn, do you want to go out for lunch today? There are a couple of good places in town for lunch and the Malt Tavern, out on the Dublin Road, puts on a really nice spread."

He smiled. "Good morning to you too. Thanks for the offer but I think I'll pass. I've become addicted to Roan canteen food and I couldn't get by without my daily fix."

"Come on. Please." Her tone was unabashedly pleading. "This won't end well. Honestly."

Her concern was touching. "Thanks, Laura. I really do appreciate the concern, but I'm not running away. I just won't."

She just shook her head sadly and picked up a document without saying another word.

That morning Finn couldn't help but chuckle at the number of invitations to lunch off campus he received. *They are all genuinely worried...and so fucking petrified.*

Eventually lunchtime rolled around. He stood up, stretched and looked at Laura. "You coming?"

Her dark eyes pooled with tears. "You don't have to do this, Finn. Really, you don't."

"Yes or no?" His tone wasn't unkind, but it brooked no more discussion.

She didn't answer but rose from her desk and headed out the door.

Finn shrugged his shoulders, followed her and they walked to the canteen in silence. As soon as he entered the canteen, conversations ceased and it felt as if the air had been sucked completely out of the room. It seemed that by just him turning up for lunch, people had concluded that he was there to fight.

Once he had paid for his food, he heard a couple of calls of, "Finn, come join us over here," but mostly everyone stayed silent and tense.

He walked purposefully over to Julia's table, keeping a neutral expression on his face and his eyes straight ahead.

"Hi, it's me again," he said brightly as he sat down at the table. "Can't beat it," he inclined his head toward his tray, "Irish stew with heaps of French fried potatoes. Doesn't get any better than this."

Julia didn't respond or even acknowledge his presence.

"Hey, what's up? Cat got your tongue?"

She lifted her head and stared at him fiercely.

Those eyes....Jesus, I could look into them all day, every day.

"Here they come. Now you've gotten what you were asking for. I hope you're happy."

Finn turned around and as she had said, the idiots who had warned him off on Tuesday were striding towards them.

"What the fuck did we tell you about sitting at this table with this bitch? And yet, here you are again, moron. Don't you get it? You're not allowed to sit here. Period."

For a minute Finn said nothing; he just looked back at them. Then his expression slowly changed, a look of surprise spreading across his face. "Wait a minute." He shook his head doing his best to appear confused. "Hold on, you guys meant all that stuff? Really? Jesus, I figured this was some kind of initiation prank for the new guy." He shrugged and grinned sheepishly. "I mean, honestly, this wasn't a joke? I swear, I really didn't know." He shook his head again, as if trying to grasp a difficult concept. "You were actually serious?"

The three guys looked at each other in puzzlement. Finn had either done a very convincing job of acting all innocent and bewildered or they were dumber than they looked.

"Yes, we were serious," one of them said. "Very serious. So fucking serious that you've created a whole heap of shit for yourself which you will very much regret, if you're lucky enough to have the opportunity."

Finn put both hands out, palms up. "'Honestly. I swear I thought this was all a put on. I wouldn't have sat here if I'd known it was *really* against the rules. Seriously. I don't want any trouble. I'm just here to do a job. I spent eight years in college to give myself the opportunity to get this job. I'm not going to throw all that away by being stupid. Anyway, I'm just one guy. What could I do all by myself?"

The leader of the three leaned in close. "Listen to me, motherfucker. If you're screwing with us you're dead. You got that? This is your last warning. You fuck around once more on anything and that's it. You got that?"

Finn nodded, attempting to appear contrite. "Yes, yes I do. And thank you, it won't happen again. I promise." He stood and picked up his lunch, as if making to leave.

"It better not." Smugly satisfied, the thugs swaggered out of the canteen.

Finn looked at Julia, winked and sat back down. "That was just to make sure they really lose the rag the next time I piss them off. Can't wait for that."

Julia looked astonished. "You're nuts. Certifiably nuts. You had me believing there that you genuinely thought this was a joke and that you were being set up. Seriously, why would anyone play a joke like that? It's nonsensical and yet they seem to have bought it. And now you say you were just winding them up more. What, they didn't look mad enough to you already? Nuts, I tell you, definitely nuts."

Finn laughed. "Wow, that's the most I've heard you say in one go. Well think of it this way, our lunchtime companions got to see a really good show and now they may actually believe it's all over and done with. The next episode should be even more fun."

Finn was right, the atmosphere in the canteen had changed considerably. The tension in the air that could have been cut with a knife was gone and overly loud conversations had replaced the eerie silence.

Finn pushed his lunch aside. "Come out with me tomorrow night, please. Let's go for a walk or a movie or dinner or whatever. We can drive to wherever you want and go from there."

Julia said nothing at first and he could tell she

was struggling with her composure. "I'm not ready for a relationship." It was almost whispered and her lower lip quivered. "I can't. I'm sorry."

"I understand." Finn gave her a warm smile. "Honest, I do. No strings attached. Let's not talk about relationships or expectations. I'm just asking you to hang out with me for a few hours tomorrow night. That's it."

"Can I sleep on it? If you need an answer now it will be 'no' but if you let me sleep on it, it might be 'yes'. I'm not promising anything, mind you."

"Absolutely." Finn beamed at her. "Absobloodylutely."

They chitchatted for the remainder of the lunch and he was pulled deeper and deeper into the spell that was Julia Davis.

Back in the office afterwards, Laura stared at him skeptically. "No way are you done."

Finn said nothing.

She shook her head. "No way. You're just building up to something bigger, I bet."

Finn just smiled. *You won't have to wait long to find out.* He was feeling very pleased with himself indeed. His plan had worked beautifully and he had snagged a date with Julia. *Almost snagged a date,* he reminded himself. *It's not a done deal yet.* And then there was the small part of him who worried that even if she did say yes, when she found out what he'd done, how he'd failed, she wouldn't want anything to do with him.

The rest of the day passed uneventfully and he put himself through a very heavy workout session that evening. "Tomorrow's another day," he said aloud as he settled in for the night.

~ * ~

Julia lay awake in her bed unable to sleep for even a moment. *What are you doing? This is so crazy.*

She chastised herself for feeling like a schoolgirl asked on a date by the star football player. She knew it could never go anywhere no matter how attractive Finn was, nor how good it might feel to have someone strong on her side for a change. Eventually, she decided she would tell him "no" tomorrow. *It's the only sensible decision.*

She lay awake all night staring morosely at the ceiling.

Chapter Seven

August, 1983
University College, Cork

Finn and his colleagues had survived the cyanide experiment in June. It had been a long day but it had been a fun day also. The whole experiment took just under twelve hours and apart from bathroom breaks and grabbing a quick bite to eat, Finn stayed in the isolation lab the whole time. He hadn't been alone there for a single minute. His lab mates and friends rallied round and took it in turns to spend an hour each with him as he attempted one of the most dangerous experiments ever tried in the chemistry department.

Throughout the day, various people popped their heads into the lab with differing reports of massive bird kills on the roof or that the emergency services were on their way and that the building was evacuated. It was all in good fun and Finn took it in his stride. When the experiment was completed, they all gathered in the bar where Finn bought several rounds.

"It's the least I can do for you gobshites. Putting your lives on the line like that. Who knew chemistry could be so exciting."

Of seemingly more danger to his health than the cyanide experiment was the series of parties that had been organized in his honor in the days before he left for Kentucky. These were serious drinking sessions that culminated four days before his departure with the age old tradition of drinking a pint in every pub on Barrack Street in a single day. This mightn't have amounted to such a big deal ordinarily, but Barrack Street, which started just a few minutes' walk from the college, stretched for almost two miles and was home to no fewer than twenty-seven pubs.

Finn knew for certain that there wasn't a hope in hell that he could accomplish this. There were stories of a few hardy souls who had successfully completed the challenge and lived to tell the tale but most participants came to an unhappy ending well before the finishing line.

"I'm definitely in the latter category," said Finn ruefully. He tried pleading to no avail to his friends that, since he was only going for six months and was returning to complete his doctorate, technically this tradition didn't apply to him on this occasion. His friends were having none of this.

"Take off your skirt and man the fuck up," Frank told him in no uncertain terms. "If you're looking for sympathy, go look it up in the dictionary. It's right there located between shit and syphilis."

"You have such a way with words. Any more wisdom you'd like to share?"

Frank smiled broadly. "Certainly. Here's another: when they release the bulls into the ring, you have to decide whether you're going to get out there and swing the red cape or be up in the stand selling tacos. And guess what, my friend, those bulls are coming for you."

And so it went on until the morning of the big day when about twelve of them gathered outside the first pub at eleven, just as it was opening up for business. They had all consumed a hearty Irish breakfast of sausages, rashers, eggs, black and white pudding and beans. This was accompanied by mounds of buttered toast and several cups of strong tea.

"You've got to line that stomach or you won't make it to four in the afternoon otherwise, not to mention to twenty seven pints," his friends assured him.

Finn groaned. He was already full and his belly felt so heavy. "Okay bitches, let's get the show on the road."

The first five pubs were pretty easy going. Finn stuck to Harp lager which he reckoned was the lightest option and far less filling than Guinness or Murphy's stout. By the time they got to number eight at about two thirty, he was really starting to feel it though. His head was buzzing, his speech was beginning to slur and his legs were getting noticeably less steady. Each time they exited a pub, the fresh air seemed to make him feel worse.

Just after four in the afternoon, they reached pub number thirteen. Finn was in a bad state by now. He had already thrown up on two different occasions and needed the support of his "so called friends" to navigate his way into the bar. He flopped in a chair, head in his hands, and would have been happy to just fall asleep there and then.

"Half ways there," Frank told him helpfully. "You're on the home stretch."

By now he was drinking two glasses of water along with every pint in a futile attempt to somehow dilute the effect of all that alcohol. Trouble was, he had consumed so much liquid already that he could feel it all sloshing around inside him and he was fit to burst. He somehow managed to force number thirteen into him and after a long break in the bathroom, staggered out to his friends.

"Your chariot awaits you outside, my lord," Kevin Burke informed him.

Finn nodded. His chariot? What the hell was Kevin was talking about?

He learned soon enough when he weaved his way out the front door. There stood a shopping cart that some of his friends had evidently persuaded a nearby supermarket to let them borrow. "We told the manager what it was for and that we'd return it intact."

"And he believed you?" slurred Finn.

"Ah, sure. Your man was a good sport. He just said you weren't to drive it drunk. So, you'll have to leave that to us."

So, with difficulty, they loaded Finn into the cart and wheeled him down Barrack Street, in and out of four more establishments, much to the amusement of passers-by and local workers.

By pub number eighteen, Finn hit a wall. He had now thrown up five times and a sixth didn't seem like it was far off. Reluctantly, his friends called it quits after showering him with insults that he barely heard because he was drifting in and out of consciousness by then.

The last think he remembered was being

wheeled back to Frank's flat, dumped on the sofa with a bucket placed near his head. He didn't wake up until two the following afternoon and he was still plenty the worse for wear for another day.

~ * ~

Now, sitting on the plane to New York two days later, he was just about fully recovered.

"No thank you," he turned down the air hostesses' many offers of wine and beer adding a silent, *never again*, each time. Once he got to New York, he had just under an hour to catch a connection to Frankfort, where he was to be met by a post-grad student from Professor Spalding's lab.

Everything was on time and he arrived in Frankfort's bustling airport none the worse for wear. After he collected his bags, he headed over to the designated meeting area where he spotted a sign with his name. He walked towards it then stopped dead in his tracks. Holding the sign above her head was a stunning, statuesque blonde about five foot ten with a figure that couldn't have been carved any better by a sculptor.

He chuckled to himself. *Man, I think I'm going to like it here*. He was already thinking of his first report back to his guy friends who had all begged him to send pictures of pretty American girls.

He started walking again until he reached the blonde. "Hi. I'm Finn. Thanks for coming to meet me."

The blonde literally gasped, looking equally as surprised by Finn as he had been by her.

"You're Finn? You're Irish Finn Lane from Cork? Holy shit, you are not at all what I'd expected." She checked him out from top to bottom without a hint of subtlety or discretion. "Wow. Are all Irish chemistry postgrads as hot as you? I am so glad I volunteered to come get you. My friends will be so pissed."

He winked. "No, unfortunately, I'm the ugly one. And you are?"

"I am so sorry. I'm Whitney. Whitney Campbell. You made me forget my manners."

Everything about Whitney Campbell was perfect as far as Finn could see. Her curly blond hair cascaded softly over her shoulders. Tantalizing round breasts, unhindered by a bra, were displayed perfectly under a thin tee-shirt that failed to conceal her erect nipples. Long, tanned legs that seemed to go on forever emerged from a tight mini-skirt. Deep blue eyes, dazzling white teeth and rosy cheeks made her face easily one of the most beautiful he'd ever seen. Even the sprinkling of freckles across her nose seemed like a perfect addition.

Finn noted she was also wearing a diamond ring on her left hand. *Engaged.*

Whitney caught his glance and in a perfectly mellifluous Southern accent, looked Finn directly in the eye with an unmistakably provocative expression and said, "Just say the word and I'll dump it in the trash can right here and now."

She held his gaze steadily until Finn could feel himself beginning to blush. "Hmm, tempting as that is, I don't think it would make either of us popular with a number of people. Besides, I wouldn't want your fiancé beating me up on my first day in America."

Whitney laughed. "Bless your heart, I guess you're right. It's probably a bit too soon for that. Anyway, just so you know, I doubt my fiancé could handle you. He might like to think so but something tells me that would be a very bad call on his behalf. Well, if we're not going to elope, are you hungry? Thirsty? I'm in no hurry to deposit you in Edgarville."

"I could stand to eat. I slept through two meal services so I am feeling a little peckish."

"Peckish, huh? As in turkeys and chickens?"

Finn laughed. "No, as in I'm starving."

"Excellent. Then I'm going to introduce you to some down home, good southern cooking." Whitney linked her arm in his, holding tight enough that he felt the swell of her breasts, causing his glance to stray back to them.

She's trouble. While she was sexy and stunning, Finn was not attracted to her physically. Still, he liked her immediately, even if her directness was a tad disconcerting.

Whitney chatted up a storm in the car. When they reached the restaurant, she insisted on ordering for him. "How does fried catfish, collards and okra sound? It's tonight's special." At his questioning look she added, "You want the full southern experience, don't you?"

It sounded far from appetizing to Finn but he merely shrugged. "Sounds great. Thanks."

She flashed a huge smile at the waitress. "He'll have the special. I'll have a salad with ranch dressing on the side."

Finn arched a brow at her. "You aren't having

the special?"

"No, I had a late lunch." She smiled up at the waitress again. "And bring us both a sweet tea."

The catfish wasn't terrible. The collards tasted a little like cabbage but they seemed to have been cooked in bacon fat. However, the okra was nearly inedible. He had never tasted anything like it. He reached for the tall glass of *sweet tea* to chase the horrible stuff and nearly strangled. Sweet tea turned out to be cold tea with so much sugar in it was nearly as sweet as syrup.

Not wanting to be rude, Finn struggled through the meal gamely. Finally putting his fork and knife down, unable to eat any more.

Whitney smiled sweetly. "I thought you said you were starving. You still have a little okra left."

"I guess I wasn't as hungry as I thought. I couldn't eat another bite."

"Finn Lane, your mama raised a nice boy, but you don't lie well."

"No really—I-I" he sputtered.

Whitney's eyes flashed with mirth. "It's okay. You did well. I wouldn't eat any of that shit."

Finn grinned at her. "This was a prank?"

"Just a little one. But I bet you have room for peach cobbler. It's really good here." She laughed at his skeptical expression. "Honestly. I'm telling you the truth. I would never lie about peach cobbler."

And, indeed, she hadn't. He quite liked the peach cobbler.

Once they were on the road again, Whitney kept up her running stream of conversation.

Finn learned that Whitney was less than a year

from completing her doctorate and had already started to write up some of her thesis. Her fiancé, Morgan Herman, was also doing a chemistry doctorate but he was in a different lab and working on very different experiments.

"We met when we were both freshmen and have been together for almost eight years now. Morgan was a star quarterback in his high school in Mississippi. Apparently, a lot of the top universities scouted him. He was a shoe-in to get a full-ride somewhere."

"A full-ride?"

"Scholarships. Enough to completely pay for college. But in the fall of his senior year, he and a friend were coming home from a party when they got into a bad car accident. Morgan had been driving and was way over the limit. He broke his leg in two places which ended his football career there and then."

"What about the other guy?"

"He was less fortunate and ended up paralyzed from the waist down. Morgan's father, who was a very successful businessman in their town, managed to keep Morgan out of jail but he was banished to KenTech as part of the deal." She shrugged.

Whitney recounted all of this in a matter of fact manner that Finn found very curious. It was as if they were discussing some distant cousin instead of the guy she was planning to marry in less than a year.

"He still has a chip on his shoulder about it." She huffed. "Actually, scratch that. He has a chip on both shoulders. He's generally pleasant but watch out for him when he's drunk, which is ofter. Then he has a bad temper and can be downright mean."

Finn looked at her. She was this gorgeous woman who clearly any man would love to be with. And yet she had just painted an extremely unflattering picture of the man she'd been in a relationship with for a big chunk of her life and who she was seemingly going to marry. He found it all very strange and was curious now to meet the infamous Morgan Herman.

Conversation drifted to other topics and two hours later, Whitney dropped him off at the well-appointed, single bedroom apartment that had been leased for him. It was far better furnished than any student accommodation he had come across in Ireland.

"This is really close to the college. You can catch the local bus at the corner, or if you prefer, you can bike it in about ten minutes—you'll have the use of one for the six months you're here. It should be here somewhere." She opened a closet by the front door. "Yup, here it is."

"That's great—really thoughtful."

She shrugged, giving him another appreciative appraisal. "We do it for all visiting post-grads but I suspect you may be the first one who'll actually use it."

Finn wasn't sure what to say so he remained silent.

"Anyway, I'll collect you in the morning and get you oriented. I can't wait to show you around. Trust me. You are going to cause some stir."

Again, Finn was speechless.

Whitney flashed her perfect teeth at him and tossed her hair back. "Now is there anything else I can do for you tonight?"

"Not tonight. You've been so generous already. Thanks."

"Well, if you're sure. Sweet dreams. I won't come get you until about eleven, so sleep in. There's food in the fridge and in the cupboard, enough to get you through a week or so. After that, you'll have to fend for yourself."

Finn smiled. "I'm sure I'll be able to manage. Thanks again. See you tomorrow."

After she left, Finn decided he wasn't tired and set off on the bike in the direction of the college to do some exploring. It was a warm evening and it seemed like half the people who he saw were students on bikes. The campus itself was amazing. It consisted of a large number of classically designed, domed red-bricked buildings, evenly spaced. The lawns and grounds were pristine and there were flowers and shrubs everywhere. Despite the bustle of large numbers of students milling about, Finn couldn't see one single scrap of litter anywhere.

Not like home. I must send pictures. They're going to be so pissed off. He smiled at the thought of the reaction that Whitney's photo would generate and wondered if some of the lads wouldn't now make do on their promises to come visit him when they saw it. That alone would be enough of an incentive for a few of them to get their asses over to visit.

Chapter Eight

Friday, June 27, 1986
Week One: Day Five

At eight-thirty that morning, Finn called in sick to Roan. He felt bad doing it on his first week but he rationalized to himself that current circumstances dictated such action. He went back to bed for a few more hours sleep to maximize his rest. It was a measure of his calmness and composure that he could actually sleep given the day he had ahead of him.

By 12:20, he was in his car driving out to Roan's facility. He parked, walked directly to the canteen and walked straight over to Julia's table. He smiled and sat down. "Hey, I thought I'd swing by to see if we're on for tonight?"

Around him the canteen reacted initially with gasps and then an eerie silence fell.

So many emotions flitted across Julia's face it was impossible to even guess what she was thinking. Eventually, she spoke. "What—Jesus Christ, Finn—what are you doing? You won't make it alive to tonight."

"Now, now, that's not a positive way of looking at things." He smiled, but was acutely aware of a group of about five or six men heading his way. He stood up and turned to face them. This time he didn't feign civility. "What do you pussies want now? Fuck off. I'm tired of this shit. If you want me, let's go outside right now and settle this. Come on, all of you. Let's go."

They just sneered back at him and one of them said, "No need for us to do anything, motherfucker. You'll be taken care. Today. You just signed your own death warrant, you ignorant prick."

Finn just stared back him. "I'll tell you what. As soon as I deal with whoever you chicken shits are sending to do your dirty work, I'm going to come and take care of you. Fucking pussies. Hiding behind skirts. Hah, yeah, you're really fucking tough." With that Finn walked out of the canteen and headed to his office.

Laura arrived breathless two minutes later.

He looked up at her. "What happens now?"

"What happens now is that you get in your car and drive and don't stop until you get to Cork. That might not even be far enough. You hear me? Go now, while you still can."

"And if I don't go? What happens then?"

"Then a gang of five of the meanest sons of bitches you'll ever encounter will come out here on motorbikes and with their baseball bats will beat you until there's nothing left of you to bury. And no one will stop them either. Not the police. No one. So go now...please, Finn. Just go."

Finn shook his head. "You know I'm not going to do that. I worked hard all week to create this situation, I'm not going to walk away now."

"Well then, you'll more than likely die a horrible death this afternoon or wish to fuck you had by the time they're finished with you." Her voice was surprisingly calm.

"Don't count on it. You're not getting the office to yourself just yet."

Outside the door of the office, the corridor was lined with people, all talking in hushed tones. Work had definitely stopped for the day.

"Thank God it's Friday afternoon," Finn said with a wry smile.

Just then the roar of motorbike engines could be heard and silence descended. He grinned. "Better not wait for them to come in and damage the furniture, so off to the lion's den we go."

With that he walked out of the office, past the lines of people who just looked at him blankly and out the door into the bright, afternoon sunshine. Just as Laura had said there would be, standing about thirty feet in front of his building were five big, mean looking guys, swinging baseball bats.

"Thought you were a big shot, huh?" one of them asked. "Thought you didn't have to comply with the rules, didn't you? Well, asshole, this is where all your thinking got you and now you're going to find out what happens to fuckers like you."

Finn walked forward until he was about eight feet from them. Two of them rushed at him swinging their bats. Finn waited until the last split second before contact, then pivoted and used their motion against them. In the blink of an eye, he caught hold of the two baseball bats, twisted strongly and wrenched them from their holders' grips. He then swung both bats at their heads, connected and watched them fall.

Before anyone could react, he swung the bats again and connected with two hands which resulted in the bats they held being dropped to the ground. He turned around quickly and smashed the bats into the heads of the first two guys on the ground, who were trying to pick themselves up. They went down with a thud and then he was back in an instant facing the other three, only one of whom had a bat.

Now he let fly as he put his years of mixed martial arts and hand-to-hand combat training to good use. He whirled, he twisted, he spun but mostly he just hit, again and again and again. Soon, all five were lying on the ground groaning in agony. Finn turned away, strode into the building, glancing at the line of shocked colleagues who'd been glued to the window. Julia wasn't among them, so he made his way to her office. He found her sitting there, in complete silence, staring blankly at her desk.

"Come with me quickly," he said.

She got up in stunned amazement and he led her into an empty conference room and over to the window. She gasped when she saw the five thugs lying on the ground in a bloody mess.

"Were any of these involved in your assault? Tell me, if they were."

She nodded and pointed out two. "What are you going to do?"

"Watch," he said and left the conference room.

Finn jogged down the hall out through the double doors. Picking up an abandoned baseball bat, he approached one of the men Julia had identified. He was curled up, clutching his abdomen and had blood oozing from what looked like a badly broken nose.

"Like to rape innocent girls, do you, motherfucker?" Finn snarled. "Well, you've raped your last." With that Finn kicked him repeatedly in the groin with all his might. The man squealed like a pig until he passed out.

Then Finn went to the second man Julia had identified and systematically beat him with the bat. He could hear bones crunching but he kept going until that one too had passed out.

When he finished, he was sweating profusely and the baseball bat was almost molded to his hands, such was the strength of the grip he had on it. He flung the bat away and looked at his five badly beaten assailants.

"Not so tough now, are you?" Finn laughed contemptuously. "You messed with the wrong guy. Tell the others I'm coming for them."

He went back into the building. No one said or did anything. In fact, everyone looked pale and immediately put their heads down if Finn looked at them.

Can't blame them, I suppose. It must be very distressing. He looked around for the canteen thugs but, not surprisingly, he could not see them. *No worries. Plenty of time for them.* For now, he needed to get out of here. He walked back out the building, headed to his car and drove away. As his adrenaline waned, he started to feel his own injuries. In fact, he was hurting quite badly. Although the five thugs had clearly come off worse, they had not gone down without a fight and Finn had taken his fair share of licks. He'd be fine, but now he needed help.

He was now a marked man, since the leaders of the gang would put a price on his head. He couldn't risk facing more of them until he had recovered a little. So bypassing the rented house where he had stayed all week, he headed out of town towards Clonafoy. About three miles down the road, he turned down a small lane that led to a picturesque farmhouse. He had taken the precaution of renting this place also when he first got to Lissadown.

Once inside, he sank into the couch. "I knew this was a good call," he said aloud. He closed his eyes, intending just to rest a few minutes, then get a bath started.

When Finn woke up it was still light outside but he could tell that dusk was coming. He ached all over and every slightest movement made it worse.

"Fuck. I'm late. First date and I can't even be there on time. Asshole."

He went into the bathroom, looked in the mirror to survey the damage. There was only minimal bruising on his face but his torso was completely black and blue.

He smiled wryly. "Oh well, at least my pretty boy looks haven't been damaged."

He didn't have time for a bath, so he splashed some water on his face, smoothed down his close cropped hair and painfully made his way to the car. He drove steadily towards Lissadown aware that he was taking a big risk. There would likely be a posse out looking for him. He also figured there was a distinct possibility that Julia's house might be watched.

"You never know though with these assholes.

They might not have put that particular two and two together."

Still, he'd have to be vigilant and, in a way, he was almost glad that it was beginning to get dark. He parked his car a couple of blocks away from her house and made his way slowly there, keeping a close watch each step of the way. He waited a good five minutes at the end of her street before approaching her house and when he did he knocked on the door quietly. When she opened it, he entered quickly, shutting the door behind him.

~ * ~

Julia had been totally distraught. Like everyone else, she had watched the destruction that Finn had wrought upon the five gang members with amazement. The level of violence he was capable of was stunning and more than a little frightening. She had been particularly touched when he zeroed in on the ones who had attacked her and she had even smiled when she saw what Finn did to them. It didn't take away the pain of what they had done to her away but, for the very first time, she felt like that she, at least, had gotten some justice.

Immediately after the fight though, she began to worry about Finn's safety. She knew this was not going to be let go unanswered. At that moment also, she had decided that she would go out with him that night. It was the very least she could do for him. It's not often someone takes your side in that way.

Julia had gone directly home after work and tried to figure out what she would wear. She had almost forgotten what it was like to dress up and feel good about herself and for the very first time in a long time she took a bath. She had completely avoided taking baths since her attack. She preferred quick showers so as to avoid as much as possible seeing her scarred and burned body. *Progress. It doesn't mean I'm pretty but being less ashamed is definitely progress."*

She dressed carefully, nothing too revealing, of course, but enough to make Finn want to take a second…and maybe a third look. After she'd applied her make-up—again another first for a very long time—she sat back in the chair feeling the butterflies awaken in her stomach.

"I need a drink. Just one to calm me down."

He should arrive in twenty minutes.

An hour later, she was still sitting alone, waiting, as she became more and more worried. She drove to his house. His car wasn't there and the house seemed empty.

She drove to the local hospital and not finding him there, finally called the police, all to no avail. Dejected and upset, she drove home and sat in the dark, crying.

She was sad for herself that yet another opportunity at happiness seemed to have disappeared but mostly she was worried about Finn. She had good reason to fear the worst and she was becoming more and more convinced that Finn had met the same fate as her brother, Brian.

Then there was a knock at her door.

~ * ~

Finn had waited a good five minutes at the end of her street before approaching her house and when he did he knocked on the door quietly. When she opened it, he entered quickly, shutting the door behind him. He'd guessed that Julia would be very pissed, though in his defense, she technically had not confirmed that she'd go out with him. He was also counting on the afternoon's excitement as mitigating circumstances. All in all, this might work out.

He was wrong. Very wrong.

"What the fuck are you doing here?" Julia screamed at him.

If he had any illusions about how angry Julia could get, they were quickly dispelled.

"Well?" Her tone was menacing. "What are you doing here? Does hero boy think he can just waltz over here now late at night and expect to get laid? So, did you think I'd be so grateful to you that I'd put out immediately? Well, you know what? Go fuck yourself. For that matter, go fuck anyone you want because let me be very clear here, you're not fucking me. Not tonight, not tomorrow. Not ever. Now get the fuck out of my house."

"Hey, look, that's not fair." Finn tried to reason with her. "I'm sorry I was late. I fell asleep on the couch and I only woke up a short while ago. I came straight here. I'm not looking for sex. I don't even know where that came from. I know it's too late to go for a walk but I wanted to come and explain. I'm sorry, okay?"

"So you were asleep for the last few hours?" Her voice dripped with sarcasm. "All alone on your couch were you?" Well answer me this, asshole; how come your car wasn't in the driveway and there was no sign of anyone in the house?" She stared at him and laughed bitterly. "Oh yeah. I'm the idiot who went over to see if you were okay. I'm the one who hung around outside your house for over two hours getting more and more worried about you by the minute. I didn't know if I should go to the hospital, the morgue, the cops. So I just sat there, crying my eyes out wondering if you were alive or dead."

Finn was speechless. He'd never imagined that *she'd* be worried about *him*.

Her eyes filled with tears and her lower lip quivered. "Don't say anything. Just go. Now. Get the fuck out of my house."

She went looking for him. He never imagined she'd do that. But if he'd given it a moment's thought, he'd have realized it was exactly what she'd do. He stared dumbly at her for a moment, wondering if he should tell her about the second house but decided against it. The less she knew the safer she'd be.

"I'm sorry," he whispered. "Really sorry. You're the last person I'd want to hurt."

"Yeah? Well too late," she retorted bitterly.

Finn looked at her for another moment then opened the door and walked outside. He checked in both directions but the coast seemed completely clear. What a total fuck up.

He was sincerely touched that she had come to check on him and he could tell her distress was genuine. He was also, ironically enough, impressed by the how angry she could get. He chuckled. "Not one to mess with, no sireeebob!"

He reached the car and made it back to the

farmhouse without encountering anyone. In fact, the streets of Lissadown were basically deserted.

"Wow, a very quiet Friday night here in the hometown. Wonder why?"

Back at the farmhouse, he made himself a sandwich and opened a beer. He had stocked the fridge with provisions a week ago so he was all set for a while. There'd be no work out tomorrow or for several tomorrows. He knew there was nothing broken but there was still going to be a lot of pain as his body recovered. He smiled to himself. "Now, what have you got to complain about boyoh? You should see the other guys."

He was tempted to turn on the TV to see what the news reports were but decided against it. "Time enough for that. Time enough."

He got himself another beer from the fridge and sat there thinking about the likely fallout and his next moves. His mind drifted to Julia. He knew while he had a lot of making up to do there, it was her concern and worry about him that had made her react the way she did. He raised his bottle. "Here's to you, Hellcat. One more beer then off to bed."

He was asleep almost before his head hit the pillow.

Chapter Nine

Saturday, June 28, 1986
Week One: Day Six

Finn was awakened by a persistent knocking on the front door. At first, he couldn't place where the noise was coming from then realized it was from the door. *Julia.* A slow smile spread across his face at that thought. Then he caught himself when he remembered there was no way she could possibly know he was here. "Who the hell could it be so?" he asked the empty room as he pulled on his pants and a tee-shirt.

He went downstairs and opened the door. Standing there was a large, distinguished looking man in a police uniform.

"Are you Finn Lane?"

"Yes, I am."

"I'm Chief Superintendent Mike McGill. May I come in?"

Finn looked at him warily. "How did you know I was here?"

McGill smiled. "Well now, Dr. Lane, I didn't make Chief Superintendent because of my pretty face. Can we talk inside, please?"

Finn stepped aside. "Be my guest."

Finn showed him into the living room. "Can I get you anything? To be honest you woke me up and I could murder a cup of tea."

The superintendent made a show of looking at his watch, shook his head and tut-tutted. "Rough night?" The hint of a smile played on his lips and his dark eyes twinkled.

"No, the night was fine. The day was a bit of a slog though."

"Well, in that case, a cup of tea would be grand. Milk, no sugar."

"Got it," said Finn as he headed for the kitchen. He couldn't help but wonder what the fuck was going on. If the *Chief Superintendent* were only here because of the fight, he wouldn't be sitting down to tea. *What does this bozo want?*

He made the tea, walked back into the living room, handed a cup to his guest and sat down. "To what do I owe the honor of a house call by the Chief Superintendent himself?"

"Oh, you know, just routine. I always make a house call when somebody comes to Lissadown and basically blows the whole town up within a week. It's kind of a tradition for me." Then his eyes narrowed and his expression became serious. "Young man, you and I need to speak. We're going to have a heart to heart and you're going to start at the very beginning and take me through this whole story, every single step of the way. If I don't think you're being honest or totally forthcoming, then your ass is mine and I'll make you pay in a way those idiots you beat up never could. Are we clear about that?"

Finn looked at him steadily for a moment or two. "You know, Chief Superintendent Mike McGill, the thing I'm not clear about is why you're here harassing me when I was clearly the aggrieved party instead of being back in Lissadown rounding up the thugs who have made the town a no-go for the past few years? *That's* the thing I'm not clear about. Or is it that the cops are too afraid of these guys to stand up to them so instead do their dirty work for them? Maybe you're here to finish off the job they failed to do. Is that it, Chief Superintendent?"

McGill's face reddened and Finn could see that he was visibly struggling to keep his composure. *Fuck him. Who does he think he is prancing in here and laying the strong arm on me. I know I'm right.*

After a thirty second staring match between the two of them, McGill sat back and took a sip of tea. "Okay. Let's back up and start again shall we? I'm not here for a confrontation with you. In fact, I'm here because I'm personally very impressed with what you did yesterday and in my personal opinion those bastards only got what was coming to them. I didn't mean to come off in such an aggressive manner. I also think, as difficult as it was to hear you say it, that you're not entirely wrong. We haven't done a great job of protecting our citizens from that mob and I'm not proud of it. So, can we push the reset button and start again in a more civilized manner?"

Finn nodded. "Sure. Let's do that."

Over three hours later, Finn walked the Chief Superintendent to the front door, looked him directly in the eye and firmly shook his hand.

"I'll be in touch," McGill said. "You take care now."

Finn shut the door and walked back into the living room. "Hmm...interesting. The plot thickens."

He spent the rest of the day and night on the couch nursing wounds and watching television. Even after several painkillers he was really suffering. *If anyone comes for me now I'm completely fucked.* He just hoped that McGill would be as good as his word. "We will see, I guess, we will see."

Chapter Ten

June, 1985
Twelve months earlier
Lissadown

Chief Superintendent Mike McGill sat in his office staring coldly at the man sitting across the desk from him. Joe Delany was a low-life thug. He was also the Assistant Attorney General for Athlone and surrounding regions.

"I know you're dirty Delany, and so help me I'll find that link to those bastards who are ruining this town."

Delany sat back in his chair, a sardonic smile on his face. An intensely ugly little man with a big head and a narrow body, he dressed shabbily and personal hygiene was not his strong suit. *As dirty as he smells*, one of his colleagues had remarked about him once. He was widely despised in the office where he worked and by all he came in contact with.

Still, what he lacked in style, Delany made up for in cunning. He had worked his way up to this position by wheeling and dealing and he certainly was not one to be crossed. McGill was fishing, and clearly Delany knew it.

"Why Chief Superintendent, I'm shocked by these baseless accusations." Delany's voice was thick with sarcasm. "I suppose you have evidence to back up such fighting words? Otherwise," he continued as his voice turned deadly cold and a venomous look came across his face, "I *strongly* advise you be very careful and fully think through the consequences of your words. Because such words could lead to consequences that you would undoubtedly regret."

"Is that a threat?" McGill was furious. "Is it? Do you know who you're talking to?"

"Now, now, Chief Superintendent, I wouldn't dream of threatening such a senior officer of the law, and certainly not one as *powerful* as you are." His tone suggested that he believed McGill had no real power at all. "Consider it just friendly advice, that's all." He stood up to leave, staring McGill directly in the eyes. "These are dangerous times, Chief Superintendent McGill. Very dangerous times indeed. A lot of things can happen in such times. Best to be very careful. Yes, best to be very careful, indeed." Delany's threat was clear and delivered with such impunity, he smiled smugly as he walked out.

After he was gone, McGill sat there fuming. He knew he'd lost that particular encounter but he also knew that he would do everything within his power to prove that Delany was dirty and on the gang's payroll.

"I'll get you, you rotten son of a bitch," he promised. "No matter what it takes, I'll get you."

These days, he felt very old, very tired and very disillusioned. He could feel Lissadown slipping deeper and deeper under the gang's control with each passing month. He had to rustle up the courage and the energy for one last battle. He needed help but didn't know where to look for it.

~ * ~

Later that night, Delany met with the four top gang leaders. "McGill is on to me. He as much as accused me today of being on your payroll."

One of them laughed. "Relax, McGill's a pussy. He doesn't have the balls to do anything. What did you say to him?"

"I told him straight out to be very careful about making accusations. I still think he needs to be sent a message."

The gang leader nodded. "Maybe you're right. We'll take care of it. I never liked that fucker anyway."

~ * ~

The next day as Sarah McGill, the Chief Superintendent's only daughter, was leaving work at the local hospital, heading home to her husband and young daughter, two men approached her. They pulled her into a waiting car and drove to a deserted car park.

"You pass on a message to your old man," one of them said as he punched her in the face. "If he tries to fuck with us both you and your brat of a daughter will be found at the bottom of Loch Ree. You got that?" He punched her hard again, opened the door and pushed her out. "You were lucky this time. The next time won't end as well for you. Make sure you tell him now."

Sarah drove directly to her parents' house.

"Jesus Christ almighty," her father exclaimed

when he opened the door and saw her bloodied face. "Did he do that to you? I'll brain the bastard!" Sarah's dad detested her husband and would be more than willing to believe he'd harm her.

"No, dad," she sobbed, sinking into his arms.

After she told him what had happened, put his head in his hands. She'd never seen him look so beaten. He was clearly devastated. "I know who did this. Those bastards, they'll stop at nothing."

Seeing her father like this scared her almost more than the thugs had. "Dad, what am I going to do? What if they go after Jane?"

He visibly steeled himself, once again becoming the father who would protect her from any bad thing. "Don't worry. I can handle this, but I'm going to have to get you out of harm's way."

"No, Dad. I don't want to leave. This is my home. My job is here."

"I'm sorry, sweetheart. I won't risk putting you and Jane in danger. Even if I back off the bastards for now, there's no guarantee you'll be safe." He gathered her in his arms. "I'll do whatever it takes to protect you."

Chapter Eleven

April, 1981
Five Years Earlier
Cork City

Finn watched the girl of his dreams from across the crowded bar. He and David had decided to go and have a few pints in a favorite pub of theirs in Cork's bustling city center. As usual the place was crowded. It was generally a young person's pub and was a regular haunt for students and those who still wanted to be students.

He couldn't take his eyes off of her. *You are so beautiful...and so with someone else.*

David Kirk followed Finn's gaze and found the girl. "Go for it," he urged. "She's cute."

"She's got a boyfriend."

"I don't see anyone with her."

Finn smile wryly. "He's gone to the loo."

At that moment, the girl looked up and her eyes met Finn's. She gave him a brief smile and cocked her head in an inquisitive manner. Did she remember him or was she just flirting?

David grinned at him. "You're on. You saw that look. Go on. What are you waiting for?"

Finn turned to him "Not going to happen my friend. We both know that."

"Careful, you'll end up with Margo if you don't watch out. She's my sister and I love her but you do not want to do that to yourself."

Finn looked back at the girl who was now arguing with her returned from the bathroom boyfriend. He was gesticulating a lot and pointing his finger over at Finn.

David frowned. "Oops, I guess boyfriend is the jealous type and has figured out that his girlfriend fancies you more than she does him."

"Stop. That's not true but I wish it was."

Her boyfriend seemed to get madder and madder and eventually jumped up from his seat, pointed over at Finn and started to walk their way.

David chuckled. "He cannot be fucking serious. Man is he in for a shock."

They both watched the boyfriend make his way through the throng of drinkers. When he was within eight feet of Finn and David, he slowed down then stopped completely. Finn stared evenly at him and could imagine the mental readjustments he was now making once he was right in front of the two of them rather than seeing their heads across the bar. Discretion overcame valor, the guy lost his nerve and turned back towards his girlfriend.

Finn looked over at her and shrugged his soldiers with a "what can you do?" expression on his face.

She responded in similar fashion and then turned and gave her embarrassed boyfriend a withering look.

Finn nudged David. "Let's go. I think that was enough excitement for tonight."

"My friend, the night is but a pup." David put his arm across Finn's shoulders. "We'll get you laid yet, no matter how difficult it is or how reluctant you are."

"Yeah, yeah," Finn growled. "I think right now I'd settle for a burger. Let's get something to eat. Almost as good as sex."

"You have a warped mind, Finn Lane." David laughed. "Either that, or you're still a virgin and haven't a clue what you're talking about. Which is it?"

Finn didn't answer him. He glanced her direction one more time. She was clearly not speaking to the very contrite boyfriend. He was half-tempted to go over and ask if everything was all right but he knew that would inflame the situation so he decided against it. "A burger it is," he said as he punched David in the arm. "Come on man, move your ass."

Chapter Twelve

Sunday, June 29, 1986
Week One: Day Seven

The four men at the meeting in the large house just on the edge of town were all livid. One of them however, the leader, was apoplectic. A large, purple vein protruded from the right side of his forehead and the blood could literally be seen pulsing through it.

These were the top men in the criminal gang that ruled Lissadown. They were all related and all ruthless. However, three of them knew that there was, in reality, only one boss—the one they deferred to here. They also knew that family or no family, if they ever messed with him, he'd have them taken out just as quickly as he would anyone else.

"What's the latest?" the leader growled.

One of his henchmen coughed nervously. "Not good, boss. Not good. They're all banged up badly. Gerry will never get it up again. Mikey won't be walking until Christmas. They're all out for months."

The boss's eyes narrowed. "What do we know about this fucker?"

The same man responded again. "Not much, boss. We know he's from Cork. He's only been here a week or so. We also know that he's into martial arts."

"Really," the boss spat sarcastically. "We know he's into martial arts, do we? What was your first fucking clue? It wasn't the fact that he singlehandedly beat the shit out of five of the hardest men I know. It couldn't have been that, could it? We know he's into martial arts. For the love of fucking God!"

The others stayed quiet. They knew from experience that when the boss got like this, saying nothing was by far the safest course of action. The most innocuous statement or response was liable to trigger an all hell's broken loose reaction and that was never, ever good.

"I want the fucker wiped off the face of the earth, and I want it done fast. We can't afford to let anyone disrespect us like that and think they can get away with it. I don't want anyone in this town or anywhere else thinking that we might be losing control. Let's show them all we are still in charge. Put a contract out on him today. Make sure you get a real professional and make sure he does the job properly. We'll pay top price. No problem there."

"Okay boss, we're on it." The three men got to their feet and hurriedly left, each of them secretly relieved to be out of the line of fire.

"Jesus," one of them said, "I've never seen him so angry. Did you see the vein in his temple? I thought it was going to burst it looked so swollen."

"Who are we going to get to do the job?" another asked. "You heard him. It better be done right."

"I know someone who knows someone in Dublin," said the third man. "It won't be cheap but I can set it up. He said money's no object so let's hold him to that. The sooner this is taken care of, the sooner things will go back to being normal."

~ * ~

"Of course I will, my dear, I'd love to." Mike McGill laughed down the phone to his four year old granddaughter who had just asked him if he would take her fishing. He and his wife called their granddaughter every Sunday afternoon without fail ever since she and her mom had moved to London almost a year ago now. They missed their only daughter and grandchild terribly and it broke their hearts to be apart from them.

"And Granda, when we catch a big fish, I'm going to bring him home, put him in a bowl and keep him as my pet. Mom won't let me have a doggie or a kitten so I'm going to catch a fish instead."

"Now honey," McGill said tenderly, "it's not mommy who won't let you get a puppy or a kitten, it's just that those are the rules where you live. I'm sure mommy would love a puppy. She did when she was your age."

When Sarah was beaten up a year earlier, her husband, Anthony, had blown a gasket on him. "You fucking idiot. What possessed you to cross those sons of bitches? Chief Superintendent, my ass. You're about as much of a threat as a toothless lion. Now you've put us all in danger." But that was about the extent of Anthony's concern for his family. Within the week he'd done a runner and was now in the States.

As much as McGill had hated doing it, he'd

sent Sarah and Jane off to London for safety. He had begged his wife to go as well but she had flat out refused.

"My place is with you," she told him each time he broached the topic. "For better or for worse. You do remember those words, dear, don't you?' He was secretly relieved that she hadn't gone but always felt guilty about that too.

"What name are you going to give your fish, Jane?"

There was silence for a moment. "Freddie. I'm going to call him Freddie," the little girl said triumphantly.

McGill was amazed at how quickly she'd picked up an English accent. There less than a year and already sounding like a native cockney. "That's a great name, baby girl. I really like it. Now can I speak to mommy for a minute?"

"Okay Granda. Bye bye. I love you."

A moment later, his daughter was on the line. "That child." Sarah sighed. "Where does she get those notions from? Fishing. That's all she talks about. 'I'm going fishing with my granda' she's been telling all her friends lately. Anyway, how's everything there? I heard there was a big commotion on Friday. Seems like some of those idiots came out the worst for wear. Who did it to them? Is he still around?"

McGill listened to her knowing he'd have to give it to her straight or she'd keep at him. "Yes, he's still here. I went to see him yesterday and we talked for a long time. He says he was provoked and then he was attacked so he simply defended himself. Apparently, he sat at Julia Davis' table for lunch on three separate days, even after he was warned not to do it. He told me he didn't think it was fair that people should be able to dictate to him who he could and couldn't have lunch with. He claims that he's the innocent party here."

"Isn't he?" asked Sarah. "It sounds to me like he is. What happens now? They won't take this lying down. He has to know there's a price on his head."

"He's a smart man. He knows the stakes. And yes, technically he's the injured party here but I have my doubts about how innocent he is. There's more going on than meets the eye, I'm sure of it."

They talked for a few more minutes before McGill handed the phone to his wife and headed to his study. He knew they'd be talking for another hour at least.

He sat in his study and thought. Although she would never say it, he knew his wife blamed him for Jane and Sarah having to move to London.

He thought about the other families who were in the same situation. They all blamed him too.

Hell, he blamed himself. Maybe it was time to retire. Let a younger man with fresher ideas take over.

Although he had been an excellent policeman for many years and had been on the short list for the Commissioner's job for a while, the past few years had severely damaged his reputation. Given the way the gang had taken over the town and operated with impunity, he was now seen to be as weak and ineffective as his former son-in-law had accused him of being.

There were even whispers about him being on the take, such was the perceived inadequacy of his response to the gang's activity. But he was neither dishonest nor weak. He had tried to find a path that maintained the peace, but he'd lost all control of the situation once police family members began to be targeted—Sarah wasn't the only one. It became virtually impossible to get them to do their jobs under those circumstances and no one was willing to transfer into Lissadown from another location.

Now though, he knew there was an opportunity. The first blow had been successfully struck and he intended to follow it up with several of his own. He laughed. "There's life in the old dog yet."

He also knew that he'd have to look out for Finn Lane. Sarah was right. There had to be a price on his head now. He'd have to take care of that. This was job one. He reached into the drawer of his desk and took out a file holding the names and numbers of people he could turn to in an emergency. *If ever there was an emergency, this is one.*

He thumbed through the document for a while then picked up the phone and listened for a moment. His wife and Sarah had evidently ended their call, so he dialed a number. "Gerry, Mike McGill here. It's been a long time. How the hell are you? You old son of a gun."

"What can I do for you, Chief Superintendent? I assume this is not a social call."

"As a matter of fact, it's not, Gerry. So let me

get straight to the point. You know that favor you owe me from when I saved your ass years ago? Well, it's time for me to call it in. Here's what I want you to do."

McGill outlined his plan to Gerry, making sure that he understood it every step of the way.

"And they say you lost it, McGill." There was a hint of grudging admiration in his tone. "Look at you thinking two steps ahead, just like the old days. By the way, I heard about the ruckus in Lissadown. Seems like the boy has really shaken things up and now you're going to ride the wave. I think you're back in the game, McGill. Let me work the phones. I'll get back to you."

"Don't mess this up, Gerry. This is far too important."

Gerry laughed. "Capiche, skipper. I got it."

McGill sat back in his chair. "Game on." A slow smile spread across his face. "Game on."

~ * ~

An hour later, the gang boss's phone rang. "It's a Gavin McGrath for you," his wife said.

He frowned for a second, then held out his hand for the phone. "What do you want?"

"I got information for you. You need to hear this."

"Go on."

When McGrath had finished, he hung up the phone and immediately dialed a number. "Call off the hit."

"But—but—"

"You heard me. Do it. Now.

~ * ~

That evening, when McGill was relaxing with a glass of single malt while watching TV with his wife, the phone rang. "I'll take it in my study," he said as he headed out of the room.

He picked up the phone in his study. "McGill."

"Chief Superintendent, it's Gerry. Job done. Worked like a treat."

"You're sure? Like I said, Gerry, this is way too important to get messed up."

"It's not messed up," Gerry replied indignantly. "It's done. Oh and by the way, Chief Superintendent, I hate those bastards so much that this one is on the house. I still owe you a favor. And one more thing. It's good to see you finally standing up to that mob. You've been sitting on your fat butt for far too long."

"Thanks Gerry. It's a new day in Lissadown."

~ * ~

Sunday evening, Julia was sitting in her living room in the dark, nursing a cup of tea. She'd endured a miserable weekend. Truth be told, all of Julia's weekends were miserable but this one had reached epic proportions. She was mad at Finn, mad at herself, mad at the world.

"Aarrgh," she yelled, "I can't stand it."

She missed her brother so much. He had been her anchor, her best friend. He always knew what to say to her when she was in a pickle. She had come to the conclusion that she was just an unlucky person. Everything went wrong in her life all the time.

And now, just when somebody had stood up for her, been nice to her, she had pushed him away too. "How stupid can you get?"

She didn't know where he was, whether he was still in town or even if she'd ever see him again. She knew she was attracted to him. It was hard not to be, he was that good looking, but there was something about that smile of his that intrigued her. It just drew her in.

She shook her head disgustedly. "What does he want with me anyway?" She believed she was nothing but damaged goods. A guy like him didn't need to go ploughing in a rotten field. She needed to just forget it, forget him. Nothing good could come of it.

When she had finished castigating herself, she sat back and as the tears fell she sobbed with such anguish that her whole body shook. She was completely alone and her heart was hurting so much that it felt like it could burst.

~ * ~

Sunday night, Finn sat by himself thinking. He was feeling much better. True to his word McGill had sent a doctor to visit him. The doctor bandaged him up properly, gave him better painkillers and left with a stern warning to take it easy, stay off alcohol and not to drive. He also told him that he'd check back in a few days.

Finn took a sip of the beer in his hand. "Oh well, I think I deserve at least one." Plus he was planning to drive tomorrow so there went another of the good doctor's warnings.

He wondered what Julia was doing right then

and if she was still mad at him.

Probably.

He wondered how he was going to change that. He needed to climb over that wall she had erected around herself. As soon as he had the thought he shook his head. "No, it's no good climbing over it. I have to break it down. But how?" He sat back, sipped his beer and thought well into the night.

Chapter Thirteen

August, 1983
Edgarville, Kentucky

Whitney Campbell knocked on the door of Finn's apartment shortly after eleven the next morning, with a young man in tow.

"Hey, Finn. Did you sleep well?"

If she had dressed provocatively for her trip to the airport to meet Finn, then she had really upped her game that morning. She was wearing a black tank top that left very little to the imagination and the shortest pair of cut off denims that Finn had ever seen—they barely covered the cheeks of her perfectly formed ass. All of this was topped off by platform open toed, cork soled sandals that made her legs look like they went on forever. Finn had to struggle mightily to keep eyes straight and not get distracted by the show. *Eyes on your own paper, son.*

"Great. Thanks for asking."

"This is my fiancé, Morgan Herman."

Whatever picture Whitney had painted of Morgan the day before was not matched in any way by the friendly guy standing in front of Finn with his hand outstretched and a broad grin plastered on his face.

"Welcome, Finn," he said as he pumped Finn's hand enthusiastically.

Morgan, about six feet tall with an athletic

build that was just starting to soften out and give way to the creeping extra pounds that were visible on his face and belly, was a good looking guy nonetheless with kind and intelligent eyes. Finn could easily see how the very gorgeous Whitney could be attracted to him.

Finn liked him immediately. He was expecting something very different.

Whitney flashed her perfect smile. "You ready to rock and roll? It's a good thing you slept well. You're going to have a busy day."

It turned out that she was not kidding. When they reached the university, Morgan left them to go to his lab and Whitney spent the rest of the morning parading him around the postgrad chemistry labs as if he were her own personal trophy. It didn't take long for Finn to realize that Whitney Campbell was the undisputed queen of KenTech's chemistry department, something that seemed to suit her just fine and she wore her crown as if it were her God given right.

Finn had the opportunity to meet with Dr. Spaulding and map out a research plan for the next few months. But as soon as that meeting was over, Whitney showed up to take Finn to lunch. He smiled to himself; even the well-respected old professor seemed slightly intimidated by her and gave her full permission to shepherd Finn around for the rest of the day.

Although she pointed out several other restaurants as they walked across campus, she took him to the staff restaurant.

"Wow. They consider postgrads staff here?"

Whitney shrugged. "Sure. After all, we're *working* on research here—not attending classes."

It only took Finn a few minutes to realize that Whitney might be alone in that opinion. It was absolutely clear that the academics might tolerate their presence but they didn't like it. Either Whitney was oblivious to them, or just didn't care about the somewhat unfriendly looks they received. Or perhaps she just enjoyed the commotion she was creating.

Finn decided there and then that he would not dine in this particular restaurant again for the remainder of his stay at KenTech.

After the uncomfortable lunch, Whitney took him to the registrar's office so he could get his identification card that would grant him access to all of the college's facilities including the libraries, the gym and other recreational facilities. Then she showed him around the rest of the campus.

In keeping with the style of the labs, the libraries and recreational areas were exceptional. He was particularly interested in the gym, which was also fully appointed with a wide array of equipment.

"You look like someone who spends a lot of time in the gym," Whitney said as they surveyed the weight and cardio equipment. "I like to work out a lot myself. Maybe we can come here together sometime? I also play a little tennis but I'm guessing that's not your choice of sporting pursuits?"

Finn smiled. "Not really. Do you just play for fun or competitively?"

"Just for fun now. But I was on the KenTech

tennis team as an undergrad. In fact, I came here on a full athletic scholarship."

"You must be really good."

She shrugged. "Not bad. I captained the varsity tennis team for back to back national championships in my junior and senior year."

"Wow. Congratulations. It seems you play more than just *a little* tennis."

She shrugged again. "I'm sort of over it. My teammates were a bunch of little bitches. They were jealous of me. I was the only girl to win a full-ride the year I came here so I got a lot of attention."

If Finn wasn't much mistaken, the attention Whitney received might have had as much to do with her looks as her talent.

"And jealous women can be so catty. I can't help it if men find me attractive while most of the rest of them…well, they weren't winning any beauty contests. At first they just bitched and moaned about the outfits I wore. Then they started making up nasty little rumors."

"About what?"

"About me and the varsity team coach sleeping together."

He arched a brow at her.

"We weren't. Frankly, I think he's gay anyway. Besides, Morgan and I had made a commitment to each other. I wouldn't cheat on him. The whole thing was just stupid."

"I'm sorry."

She waved her hand, as if batting away a pesky insect. "I'm used to it. You see, *Dr. Finn Lane, from Ireland, who seems to have everything going for him*, I'm actually a majorly fucked up girl."

Whoa. This was unexpected.

Maybe she read his surprised expression, because she jumped in immediately to explain herself. "I'm not looking for sympathy or anything, and trust me, this is not a chatting you up story. I just—well I'm not who you think I am. And when people learn the real truth, they look at me differently—like I'm a fraud. I'd rather you know from the start. I'll tell you the whole sordid story if you want to hear it."

"It can't be that bad."

"Trust me, it is. But I don't want to talk here."

He wasn't sure where this was going, but he nodded and followed her outside, into the late afternoon sunshine.

They walked in silence for a minute until they were well away from prying ears. "So, now I'll tell you the Whitney Campbell story. You may look at me and see your stereotypical upper middle-class, all American girl. Everyone does, but reality is far duller and bleaker. I come from nothing. I mean, dirt poor, white-trash nothing. I don't even know who my father was."

"That's not your fault."

"No, it's not. But it isn't like he and my mom split up or he ran out on her after he knocked her up. *She* didn't even know who he was because she was a hooker on the streets of New Orleans and he had just been one of her johns."

Finn tried not to look shocked but this was the last thing he expected her to say. A small part of him even wondered if it were true but he couldn't see why Whitney would make this up.

She smiled sadly. "Yes, in order to put food on the table, my mother walked the streets of New Orleans selling her body. Unfortunately, the ending to this ugly story is even worse." A tear slipped down Whitney's cheek. "My poor mother who tried to do her best to take care of a child she never wanted, was brutally murdered by an irate john who decided that she wasn't worth paying for after all.

Finn just sat there and listened in silence.

"I was ten at the time. It took three days before my mother's body was discovered in a dumpster with her throat slit and longer for them to connect her with me. I was by myself in our apartment for days. I had no idea what had happened. She had always come home before dawn. I didn't know what to do. There was no one I could turn to for help. The neighborhood hooker didn't have a lot of friends and Mom always warned me not to leave when she was out, and not let anyone in or talk to anyone."

She swiped at her tears and for an instant Finn saw the scared ten-year-old kid.

"So I just sat there and waited for days. I survived on cornflakes and peanut butter—the only food in the apartment. When the police finally found me I was put into the care of Child Protection Services.

"Funny, a dead whore didn't even make the obituaries, but a cute little blond girl, living on her own after her mother was killed, made the six o'clock news. I was fostered by a very wealthy, prominent New Orleans family in a matter of weeks. They'd been unable to have children of their own and were completely enchanted by the precocious little girl they'd seen on the news. My foster parents had old family money and lived in an exclusive suburban neighborhood. They even had their own tennis court on the property. I, of course, took to the game quickly and when my foster father saw that I had talent, he organized private lessons with a professional. I wanted to please him—after all, he was savior—so I practiced relentlessly. Ultimately, I was good enough to get the scholarship."

"So there is a happy ending."

"Not really. We've been estranged since I graduated from high school, but I'm not going to get into that. I haven't spoken to them in seven years and I don't want them back in my life." She appeared to steel herself, then looked him squarely in the eye. "So now, Dr Finn Lane from Ireland, you know the truth. Under this thin veneer of respectability, I'm just a whore's bastard. What do you think of me now after hearing all this?"

Finn stopped walking and put his arms around her, hugging her tightly. "I think it was very brave of you to tell me all of this and I respect you tremendously for doing so. However, everything that you told me happened *to* you. You didn't ask for any of it but you endured it. You made it though. You're tough and you need to stop thinking of yourself as a whore's bastard and see yourself as a survivor. That's what I think."

Whitney burst out crying. "Thank you for saying that. I—well, most people are willing to think the worst when they find out the truth." She stepped back from him and wiped her face. "Finn, I think this is the beginning of a beautiful friendship." She fixed a smile on her face, and just like that, Whitney was back. "Anyway, it feels good to be seen with the handsome and mysterious Irish stud who's the talk of the whole campus."

He smiled at her. "I think I should be heading home."

"Not so soon. I'll take you to dinner."

His eyes narrowed. "No thanks, you've done that already."

She laughed. "No pranks this time, I promise."

"Maybe another evening. It has been a busy day, and I'm still jet-lagged."

"Okay. I wouldn't want to interfere with your beauty sleep."

She drove him to his apartment, but once there tried again to persuade him to grab a bite or at least go for a drink.

"Really, Whitney, I'm beat."

"All right, sleepy head, off to bed with you. I'll pick you up in the morning at eight."

"That's okay, you don't have to. I'll cycle in."

She frowned and there was an awkward moment of silence, before she put on her best smile. "Suit yourself."

Chapter Fourteen

Monday, June 30, 1986
Week Two: Day One

Monday morning seemed to hit Lissadown with the ferocity of a cyclone. The town literally swayed with excitement and it felt like a strange, electric atmosphere had encircled it.

Chief Superintendent McGill had cloistered himself in his office with his top direct reports and issued instructions that they were to be disturbed only in a total emergency. There they strategized on how they could turn Friday's events to their advantage. McGill was convinced that the tide was beginning to finally turn in their favor and that now was the time to strike. His men were of the same mind. They had long been frustrated with the way things had gone and some of them blamed McGill for not dealing with it earlier. Still, getting the job was a bigger concern so they put their feelings aside and focused on the job at hand.

~ * ~

Later Monday morning, David Kirk slipped quietly in through the back door of a house in Lissadown. He had watched the occupants leave fifteen minutes earlier and knew that they would be out of the house for at least two hours. Their pattern never varied.

He smiled to himself. *I won't need half that.* He

roamed from room to room. Sure enough, less than forty minutes later, he was in his car heading to the meeting place he had arranged with Finn. When he arrived, Finn was already there.

Finn got out of his own car, walked quickly over to David's and got into the front passenger seat. "How did it go?"

"Piece of cake. No problem at all."

"Did any one see you?"

David shook his head.

Finn smiled. "Where is it?"

"In the boot. Bloody heavy too."

"I take it you got everything so?"

"Oh yeah." David laughed. "Everything and then some. I assume you'll fill me in when the time is right?"

"I will. And thanks again. I really owe you."

David frowned. "You don't owe me shit. Just take care of yourself, okay?"

"That's a promise. Now let's trade cars and you get on the road." Finn gave him a quick hug. "Say hi to your mom and Margo."

"To be sure," said David as he got out of the car.

Finn scooched over into the driver's seat and waited until David had left before driving back to the farmhouse and safely stashing what David had removed from the house.

~ * ~

That morning, in her bedroom in West Cork, Margo Kirk read the news report on the events in Lissadown with interest. Although no names were mentioned, Margo was convinced that Finn was involved. "Way to announce yourself to the town, boyoh." She laughed. "Maybe it's time to come see you."

She thought for a moment then slipped her hand into the front of her panties. "Looks like I need a wax job first. It's getting a bit stubbly down there. Can't expose the boy to that."

She let her hand linger for a moment then moved it slowly down. She was already wet when she reached her clit. She lay back in her bed, opened her legs and began to stroke herself slowly with her right hand. She moved her left hand up inside her tee-shirt until it reached her right breast. Her nipple was already taut and full as she began to caress it.

Her mind drifted to a picture of her sitting naked astride Finn Lane as she rode him hard. After a couple of minutes, she turned over onto her stomach, buried her face in the pillow, and rose up onto her knees. She stroked herself faster, more urgently as she rocked back and forth, her breathing growing shorter and shallower.

"Oh Jesus," she gasped as the wave of her orgasm hit her hard. She sank down onto the bed with her hand still between her legs.

"Oh Jesus. That was pure fucking chemical. If you can do that to me when you're not here Finn Lane, imagine what you could do if you were actually fucking me?"

She took her hand from between her legs, brought it to her mouth and licked her fingers. "Someday, my beautiful Finn, I'm going to give you the ride of your life and this taste will stay in your brain forever. And that's a promise."

~ * ~

Just after noon, Finn pulled out the driveway and headed to Roan Pharmaceuticals. "One of these days, I'm actually going to have to show up and do a day's work." He smiled wryly. "Can't keep just dropping in for lunch."

He wondered what sort of reception he would get today. He figured that Julia would still be mad at him but he also doubted that he'd get hassle from anyone. "You just never know. But we'll see soon enough."

When he arrived, he went straight to the canteen and not bothering to get any food, he walked over to Julia's table and sat down. His presence created a commotion. He'd suspected as much, but he had other concerns that were more important.

Before he could say anything, Julia reached out her hand and touched his. "I'm so glad you're here. I was worried that something might have happened to you or that you would have left and I'd never see you again. Finn, I'm so sorry. Please forgive me. I've been mad at myself all weekend."

Finn just sat there in amazement. This was not the reaction he had anticipated in any shape or fashion. He was speechless.

"Please say something. Don't just sit there. The silence is killing me."

"I-I-I'm sorry. To be honest, I'm completely taken aback. I was sure you'd chew the face off me."

Julia smiled at him. "A good surprise then. So, I'm just going to put this out there, before I lose my nerve. Do you still want to meet? Can we do it tonight?"

Finn's face split into a grin. "Yes, please. But maybe it's best if I don't show up at your house. Do you know Broderick's pub in Kilavulla?"

Julia nodded.

"Can we meet there around half past seven?"

She smiled. "I'll be there."

They sat and talked for a while until Eddie Barrett, one of the company vice-presidents, appeared at the table. "How are you, Dr. Lane? Are you doing okay?"

"I'm grand, thanks for asking."

"And how are things with you, Julia? Keeping busy?"

Finn could hardly keep from laughing. This was a pivotal moment. Clearly, just like everyone else, Eddie had ignored her for months and here now he was making a public showing of speaking to her. *What will you do, my pretty girl?* Finn half hoped she'd tell him to fuck off and by the look in her eye, the thought had clearly crossed her mind.

But she smiled, looked up at Eddie who stood there expectantly, and said, "Not too bad, Eddie. Thanks. Bit busier than I'd like to be but I'm getting there."

Unabashed relief flooded Eddie's features. "Glad to hear it. Very glad to hear it. I'll be seeing you guys."

Finn watched for a moment as Eddie left the canteen. "Well how about that? I bet you didn't see that coming."

"No, I did not."

"Well I'm off, then." Finn stood up from the table. "See you tonight."

On his way out, several people greeted him and asked if he was okay and when he was coming back to work. He stopped at Laura's table. "Hi, Laura. See you tomorrow. I'll be in bright and early."

She looked up at him. "I haven't been in all that long myself."

She did look a little worse for the wear. "What's the matter? Are you sick? Maybe you should go home too."

"Nothing's wrong with me that time and hydration won't fix."

Finn chuckled. "Rough weekend? Somehow I didn't take you for a heavy drinker."

"Normally I'm not. I went out with some friends Saturday and met a guy. We...uh...we kind of hit it off."

Finn grinned. "Ah, alcohol *and* no sleep."

She nodded. "Right in one."

"Then here's to both of us feeling better tomorrow."

~ * ~

The owner of the house that David Kirk had been in returned that afternoon. When he saw the open cabinet with all its contents removed, he knew he was in deep trouble.

"How the fuck?" This couldn't have happened. He was the only one who knew the combinations but the open locks lay on the floor. Panic flooded him. *This can't be happening. They'll assume I did it.* He went upstairs and began packing. He had to get away. He wasn't sure how far would be far enough, but if he didn't get the hell out now he was screwed. He might be screwed anyway. He couldn't think about that now. The only possible way to save himself was to disappear. *Now.*

~ * ~

That afternoon, Brendan Macken, a production operator at Roan, approached a colleague. "Hey, how are your friends doing? That was a bad beating they took on Friday. I hope they're okay."

The guy looked at Brendan as if he had lost his mind. "Are you fucking nuts? Because if you're not, you're playing with fire and likely to get burned."

Macken raised his hands innocently. "What do you mean? I was only being polite asking about your friends."

Two other men joined the first one, surrounding Brendan.

The first man clenched his fists.

"You think you can pull this shit and get away with it, do you? Think again."

"Leave him be," a voice called out.

Brendan leaned to one side, looking around the men who had surrounded him. Six or seven other production operators had taken up positions behind the others.

"Walk away now while you still can," one of them warned.

The three who had first approached Brendan glanced at each other before turning to walk away.

"This is not over," one of them snarled over his shoulder.

"That's for sure," Brendan Macken called out to their retreating backs. "You can count on that, assholes."

~ * ~

About an hour later, the gang boss's phone rang.

"Boss, I have bad news. Frankie's gone and so are all the weapons."

He went rigid. "What the fuck happened? I want his ass here…*now*."

"I'm sorry, boss, he's gone. He left a note saying someone broke in and stole everything. But he's done a scarper."

Rage rose within him, but his voice remained deadly calm. "Find him. He hasn't had time to go far."

"I put men on it as soon as I found out. But he's covered his tracks pretty well."

"Son of a bitch. Well he'd better stay missing, if he knows what's good for him. Stay on it." He banged the phone down.

This was bad. Very bad. He prided himself at maintaining complete control at all times. Nothing escaped his iron fist. But with McGill starting to grow a set and all of their weapons now missing with no real likelihood of getting replacements any time soon, the situation was rapidly spinning out of control.

Panic, something he hadn't felt in years, began to compete with his fury.

Calm the fuck down. Don't lose focus. This is only a minor setback.

He sat down, lit a cigarette and mulled over various scenarios as he smoked.

~ * ~

"I'm going to be so late," Julia groaned as she drove herself demented over what to wear. She had already tried six different combinations but none of them satisfied her. She wanted him to think she'd at least made an effort. "But I'm not tarting myself up for anyone." She stared morosely at the current outfit. Maybe she'd gone too far. The fact was, she didn't possess any clothes that could even remotely be considered for one second something a tart might wear. The outfit she had on now would look overly conservative on someone's granny.

Eventually, she settled on a red blouse and black trousers. She opened the first two buttons in the blouse then closed one up when she thought she was showing too much cleavage. "Not very appropriate for tonight," she murmured.

By the time she got to the pub, she was twenty minutes late. Finn was sitting in the corner nursing a pint with an anxious look on his face. Apart from one old man sitting at the bar, there were no other customers in the pub.

A look of relief flashed across Finn's face when he saw her. "Hey." He got to his feet. "I thought maybe you got lost, changed your mind or that I had given you the wrong time."

"No, sorry." Julia smiled apologetically. "I'm just late and I have no good excuse."

"That's absolutely fine." Finn virtually beamed at her. "What can I get you to drink?"

"Gin and tonic, please," she replied as she sat down. "Tanqueray if they have it. If not, Bombay Sapphire. Failing that, Smirnoff. Failing that—"

She grinned. "—that excuse for a gin they make down in Cork will do, as long as there's lots of tonic."

"Hah." Finn smiled at her. "Picky, aren't we? And you yourself from Cork also."

Julia's brows drew together. "How do you know that?" She had grown up in Cork, but it wasn't widely known. In fact, it wasn't known at all.

"Are you kidding me?" Finn laughed. "With that accent? Sure, where else could you be from?"

She was only partially mollified by his response. "I do not have a Cork accent." Her tone sounded more indignant than she'd intended.

It didn't seem to bother Finn. He winked at her before heading to the bar to get her drink. When he returned, she was more relaxed.

"Sláinte." He clinked his glass to hers.

"Sláinte." She took a sip of her drink then gave him the warmest smile she could muster. This was hard. Beyond hard. But in order to move on, to even have the faintest hope of a friendship with him, she had to do it. "I need to tell you about that night. It's important to me that you know exactly what happened and how I am today as a result."

"It doesn't matter to me, Julia. You don't have to tell me anything. I don't need to know."

"Please, this is very difficult for me and perhaps you don't need to know, but I need to tell you. Please." Her throat tightened and tears welled in her eyes. *Get a grip. You'll never get through it otherwise.*

Finn sat back in his seat and nodded. "Okay."

"Please, let me finish the whole story before you say anything. Can you promise me that?"

~ * ~

Finn nodded again.

And then he listened.

As she told him about Brian, regret and guilt threatened to consume him. But he suppressed the need to make his own confession. He told himself this was her moment. There would be time later.

He listened as Julia walked him through in great detail what had happened to her that night and afterwards. She described the abduction and what those men had done to her. She didn't in any way attempt to spare herself the trauma of having to say it all out loud nor spare Finn from having to hear it. And with the same strength of resolve, he listened.

At times, she had to pause and blow her nose or catch a breath or wipe away the tears that streamed down her face. Finn was glad of the privacy Broderick's offered without having to endure this ordeal in one of their homes. At times, he felt like his head was going to burst with anger while at other times, he thought his heart would break, such was the unspeakable sadness written on Julia's face.

Finn sat with her, listening to her every word, never once taking his eyes away from her face. He was absolutely amazed by the courage, determination and will to survive that this girl had shown and continued to show every day. He was totally in awe of her. There are very few people who could have endured that much punishment and still be able to sit across from someone and relive the events.

When she had finished, Julia was quiet for a moment. She took a deep breath before saying, "And that is why I have to be by myself. I'm broken and I'm no use to you or anyone else. I really like you and I'm so grateful for what you've done. Heck, you've almost given my life back. But I can't be with you as a girlfriend, not in the normal way. I was a virgin before that night. I wanted to wait until the right guy came along. Now, I don't think I can ever face sex again. I can't bear the thought of someone taking my clothes off or…or…well, I just can't. I'm sorry. I needed you to know."

Finn looked at her and said gently, "Is it my turn now?"

Julia nodded.

"Okay then. First, thank you for telling me this. I can't even begin to imagine how horrible it was for you to have to relive that night. I think you're very brave. Second, I think I let those guys off too easily on Friday. If I had known this back then, they'd have gotten far worse. Third, and most importantly, I really like you and I want to be with you." *And that was a huge understatement.* "I'm willing to accept whatever rules and boundaries you want to establish. That's fine with me. You give me a chance, please. There's no promises required nor will there be demands made."

Julia gave him a sad smile. "I know you're being honest, but seriously, how long would it last? Look at you, women throw themselves at you and you think you'll be happy with the one girl in the country who won't sleep with you. I know you'll get fed up and leave eventually and that would kill me. I could not bear for another person I care about to leave me. It's happened too often." Julia's eyes filled up again with tears and she looked down at the table.

Finn reached across, lifted her chin up and wiped her tears very gently away. "All I'm asking for is a chance. I know it's difficult but can you please give it a try? If you get concerned or anything, then walk away, but please give us just this one chance." He looked into Julia's eyes for several long moments, her warring emotions most evident there. "Please, Julia."

"God help me, but okay. Just for a trial period, mind you."

"Perfect." Finn smiled broadly at her. She smiled back. She looked exhausted and sure, why shouldn't she? She'd just run an emotional marathon. "Now, beautiful girl, it's getting late, shall we go?"

When they left the pub, it was pouring rain. As Finn walked her to her car, Julia staggered and almost fell. He wrapped his arms around her and held her closely. The fact that she leaned into his body instead of pulling away gave him joy. They stood there in the pouring rain for several minutes without speaking or moving, both of them getting completely soaked. Julia cried softly. Gentle, cleansing tears that mixed with the raindrops.

Finally, Finn took her face in his hands and kissed her forehead "I'm here. And I'm on your side. Just remember that. Okay?"

She nodded her head, got in her car and drove away.

On the way home, Finn kept thinking about what Julia had told him and how broken she believed she was. "It took a lot of guts to do that," he said aloud. "A hell of a lot of guts." In the background he could hear Leonard Cohen singing *Sisters of Mercy* in that unmistakable voice of his. Finn smiled to himself. He had always thought that Leonard couldn't sing but what a voice he had. It suited his melancholy songs so perfectly. This song was a particular favorite of Finn's, telling a story of love, loss and the road to redemption.

The song reached its pivotal moment. *That's it. Once again you hit the nail on the head, Leonard. "Graceful and green as a stem"—that's what's needed here.*

His thoughts turned to the men who had done those horrible things to her. "Two down, two to go. The next two won't get away as lightly, I promise you that Julia."

~ * ~

For Julia, the journey home was very different to her trip to the pub. On one hand, she felt as if a huge weight had been lifted from her shoulders. On the other hand, the graphic details were now out there in glorious Technicolor. She felt certain that no man, no matter how good or how understanding he was, could ever put those images aside. It just wasn't possible. She was also convinced that even if those images didn't deter someone, the sight of her completely disfigured body would more than do the trick.

"Oh well. I had no choice but to tell him and now I have to trust him."

She smiled to herself. It had felt nice when he held her. She wondered if it would ever happen again. She felt more alive than she had for a long, long time.

Chapter Fifteen

July, 1984
Two Years Earlier
Moscow, The Soviet Union

Finn and David sat across from each other in the dank and musty dressing room. They were in Moscow, both competing in the European mixed martial arts championship. This was their first time participating in the competition and they were the only Irish fighters to have made it there.

David had competed in the light heavyweight division and was beaten in the fourth round. Finn, however, had made it to the final of the heavyweight division and was now just twenty minutes away from his shot at becoming the undisputed best mixed martial arts fighter in all of Europe with a chance to fight for the world title in Brazil six months later. There was one last obstacle to overcome first though. A very, very large obstacle. His opponent in the final was Sergei Litkov, a native Muscovite and the hometown favorite.

"Man, I don't envy you," said David. "Litkov is an absolute beast of a man. Six foot six, and two hundred and seventy pounds of pure muscle."

"I know, David."

"And, he's been the undisputed champion for the last five years."

"Thanks for reminding me."

But David was right. Not only was Litkov a great fighter, he was an extremely mean fighter who set out with the intention of not just winning the bout but of hurting his opponent as much as possible.

"Do you have a plan?"

Finn frowned. "I'm not afraid of him, but to have a chance of winning I have to keep the fight going until the third round. As far as I know, Litkov had never fought beyond three minutes."

"Because everyone who has faced him is afraid of him. They go down early to save themselves a little misery."

"But that could be the answer. Stamina might be his Achilles heel. The question is, how do I stay alive long enough to tire him."

"Keep running around the ring as fast as you can."

"Funny guy. I think we need something a little more solid than that."

"Seriously, just keep moving. Ride the punches as much as you can, stay away from the ropes and whatever you do, don't let him pin you on the ground."

The door to the dressing room opened and a voice shouted, "Come now. We go start fight."

Finn and David stood up and embraced.

"I'm proud of you, man," David said. "Win or lose, I'm so fucking proud of you."

"Thanks, Dave. By the way, on the off chance that we do win, we'll need to get out of here fast. I imagine the hometown crowd will not be pleased if their hero goes down."

"All sorted. Transportation to the airport is arranged. From there we fly to Paris to go chat up all those gorgeous mademoiselles. So, try not to let your face get too bashed in. You need all the help you can get to pull one of those pretty things."

Fin grinned. "That's what I like about you, buddy. You have your priorities fully in order."

"Damn straight." David laughed. "Oh and by the way, just remember—the home town crowd may hate you but every other fighter and trainer is pulling you and hoping that you'll beat the nasty pig."

Finn knew this was true, Litkov had no friends in the mixed martial arts world but he was still the one who had to face him.

They left the dressing room and started the walk down the center aisle towards the raised ring. The room was packed, very smoky and very hot.

The raucous Russian crowd jeered at him as they chanted, "Sergei, Sergei, Sergei."

Finn reached the ring and climbed in through the ropes. The announcer half-heartedly introduced him and the crowd booed mightily when they heard his name.

Suddenly, the room reverberated with blaring music as Sergei Litkov and entourage made their way towards the ring. The crowd went mad with excitement and the "Sergei, Sergei, Sergei" chants multiplied tenfold to compete with the blaring music. Litkov jumped into the ring, pranced around a bit, and then stood silently as the ring announcer, now with passion and fervor, introduced the man of the hour.

Litkov approached Finn, glared at him and snarled something in Russian.

Finn didn't understand a word but he was sure he understood the gist. It was Litkov's common approach to strike even more fear into his opponents' hearts by abusing them in Russian, especially when he was on home soil.

Finn stared back at him equably. *Ugly fucker.* He leaned towards Litkov and said, "*Ni ceapaim go bhfuil tú go hállain.*" Finn figured telling him he was ugly in Irish was far safer than saying it in English. He felt confident that other than himself, only David Kirk would know what he meant.

Litkov snarled what was certainly another ugly Russian epithet before the referee sent them to their respective corners.

Ah yes, the referee. Finn reminded himself not to expect any help from that quarter.

The bell rang and the fight was on. Litkov charged out like a raging bull determined to end this fight just as quickly as he had all the others.

Finn though was ready. He ducked and weaved constantly, took his chances to strike when they came and generally ended up frustrating the hell out of Litkov. By the time the bell for the third round sounded, Finn's face was a mess, his left arm was useless and he was essentially hobbling on one leg. He had defied all the odds and lasted into the third round. Though Litkov was far and away ahead on points, he was visibly tiring and Finn knew this fight would not be settled by points.

Finn managed to survive another three minutes, and then his moment came. Litkov left his guard down for a split second. That's all Finn needed. He did a full three sixty degree spin and mustering every bit of power left in his body drove his foot directly into his opponent's kidney. Finn almost heard it burst there and then as Litkov fell to his knees in agony. Finn immediately smashed his foot full force into Litkov's face then jumped on top of him and started to pummel him with both fists.

Litkov had stopped trying to defend himself much too soon. *Son of a bitch.* Finn wanted to administer the kind of beating Litkov was famous for but he couldn't. He stood and stared at the now unconscious fighter. There was stunned silence in the room and the referee, who was as dazed as the audience, lifted Finn's arm in victory.

David shouted, "Yes, yes, yes." But the crowd began to rumble and objects started to land on the ring.

"Time to scarper," he shouted to David and they fled to the dressing room. Five minutes later they were in a taxi heading to the airport.

Finn sighed. "Phew, that was way too close for comfort."

"You did it. You are the top fighter in all of Europe. That's huge, man. Next stop, the world championship."

Finn sat back. As sore he was he savored the moment. "Maybe I will go to Brazil. What's there to lose? At least Litkov won't be there."

"That's for certain. In fact, I suspect Litkov will never fight again."

"And that's not a bad thing. You've heard the same stories I have, about him being an enforcer for the Russian mob."

David nodded. "Word is he's silenced many people for his paymasters."

"Well, that's unlikely to be the case going forward."

"Too bad the results of this bout won't ever make it out of Russia. You deserve bragging rights."

"It doesn't matter. It's better this way." Finn knew he'd need anonymity down the road.

A little over two hours later, after Finn had cleaned up and David had patched him up as best he could, they sat on an Air France flight to Paris. David flirted shamelessly with the air hostesses, who kept plying him with champagne.

Finn, much to the disappointment of one particular hostess, did not participate.

"Don't mind him," David said with an evil grin. "He wouldn't be much use to any of you tonight anyway. Luckily though, I can do the job of two." And so it went until they landed in Paris.

"Come on champ," David said once they had picked up their luggage. "Let's get you to the hotel. It's been a hell of a day. Tomorrow, we go the hospital and let them put you back together again."

Chapter Sixteen

Friday, July 5, 1986
Week Two: Day Five

The rest of the week had passed relatively uneventfully for Finn. For the first time he felt he was actually getting a chance to do the job he was hired and being paid for. He'd had lunch with Julia every day this week and yesterday Laura had joined them at the table for a while. This had passed off without incident and it seemed that people were gradually becoming less nervous to interact with Julia.

Tension was still high in the town but it seemed like an uneasy ceasefire had broken out. There was a higher police profile, a lower criminal profile by gang members and a few green shoots here and there of borderline normality were emerging.

Early that afternoon, his boss summoned him. He was the slightest bit concerned about why.

Once he was seated, the man gave him a stern look and without preamble asked, "So Finn, do you have a passport?"

This wasn't what Finn expected. Maybe a discussion about Roan's working hours or at best the direction of his research. But his boss was a no-nonsense guy who detested small talk and usually just got straight to the point. "I do."

The man nodded and his expression softened. "Good. There's a conference on in Lugano,

Switzerland the week after next. We've had representatives there for the last three years. I'd like you to attend this year. Obviously, we'll pay all expenses. It's also a nice spot. Mountains nearby, you're surrounded by the lake and you can drive through the Alps into Italy. The conference is Tuesday through Thursday but you should stay the weekend and come back Sunday night."

This really wasn't what Finn expected and it seemed to be a fait accompli. If Finn had had other plans, they were clearly inconsequential. Finn smiled broadly. "Sounds great. Thanks."

"Perfect. We'll get you all particulars next week. I'll expect a detailed report on the conference but not on your weekend."

Finn looked at him for a moment, a little taken aback. He could have sworn he saw a smirk on his boss's face when he made the last comment. *He's just trying to be funny. Cut him some slack. Don't be paranoid.*

Just before it was time to quit for the day, Finn bumped into Julia in the corridor.

She gave him a sort of a funny look. "How's your Italian?"

"What?"

"How's your Italian?"

"Well, I have enough to make sure that I wouldn't starve or die of thirst if I was over there."

"Excellent. You're responsible for food and drink so."

"I don't think I follow you, Julia. This is going was over my head."

She laughed. It was perhaps the first truly

happy laugh he'd ever heard from her. "Well I guess you weren't let in on the secret."

He would have been irritated had it been anyone else, but she was so clearly enjoying herself, he went with it. "Obviously not. Care to enlighten me?"

"We're going to the conference in Lugano together. It's in the Italian-speaking part of the country."

They were going together? His boss was a sly fucking cupid—and it thrilled him. He must have had looked like a gormless idiot, standing there with his mouth open.

Julia's smile faded a little. "I was just trying to be funny. Are you upset?"

"Oh God, no. I'm thrilled. I just didn't expect it." He frowned. "How do you feel about this? Are you okay? It's a bit contrived, don't you think?"

Her smile warmed again. "Of course it's totally contrived but let's talk about it later. Will I see you tonight?"

"You bet. I'll swing by at half-seven."

"Bring the vino." She grinned. "I'll cook us a classic Italian meal."

The classic Italian meal turned out be pizza from the new restaurant that had opened a few weeks earlier. Finn didn't care. He really enjoyed Julia's company. But he also accepted that their relationship was totally platonic and he knew any wrong move would totally scare her away. He had to be sure this trip to Lugano wasn't too much too soon.

After dinner, as they sat at the kitchen table

with a glass of wine each, he raised the subject again.

"So, are you okay with going to the Lugano conference with me?"

"To be honest, I'm excited and a little scared. I don't know if I would want to go if it was with anyone else." She smiled and added, "But if it was with anyone else I wouldn't be as nervous. Does that make sense?"

"It does. I get it. But you're okay?"

She nodded. "Yes. Nervous, but okay."

"Then there's something else. My boss said that I should stay the weekend. He said it's a lovely area and you can up into the mountains or drive into Italy. No pressure, but would you be interested in doing that?" He watched her expectantly as she processed this suggestion. He half thought that she'd dismiss it out of hand.

After a moment, a slow smile spread across her face. "Yes. Let's do it. But you understand the ground rules, right? Separate bedrooms. No expectations."

Yes! "Great. I got it. No expectations.

We're on the same page. Let's plan it out properly to maximize our time there."

Chapter Seventeen

October, 1983
Edgarville, Kentucky

Finn settled in quickly to life at KenTech. He was having so much fun and learning so much that, at times, he began to wonder how he would ever settle back in Cork. The days fairly flew past, until one morning he realized he'd already been there for two months. Only four months left, but he was determined to make the most of them.

He was very pleased with how his research was progressing and was convinced he'd accomplished more in two months here than he had in the previous year in Cork. He had settled into a punishing daily workout routine but he also attended enough parties to be sociable.

He particularly enjoyed going to sporting events, especially football. While KenTech was only a Division 3 school and didn't compete against any of the top teams, to Finn the whole experience of going to a game was fascinating. His colleagues patiently tried to teach him the rules and finer points of the game but he still found many passages of plays confusing.

Whitney Campbell continued her efforts to take ownership of him and even though he gave her no encouragement whatsoever, it didn't stop her from coming on to him occasionally. To his surprise, he had grown to like Morgan Herman, who if at all was jealous of the obvious attention his fiancé lavished on Finn, never once showed it.

Finn had been at KenTech for seven weeks when he learned the chemistry postgrads had a softball team that participated in a local league. While the overall purpose of the league was primarily social, the games were very competitive and taken very seriously. The chemistry team had lost their first game to the local fire department team. Finn had hoped to go see the game but an issue with one of his experiments had confined him to the lab that evening.

The team was slated to play the reigning champions from the school board in their next game. Unfortunately, the second game was scheduled on a day when four of the roster were going to be out of town at a major chemistry conference. In fact, so many chemistry postgrads were going to be away, they had no substitutes. Not wanting to forfeit the game, they turned to Finn and Paul Oxhill as last resorts.

Paul was postgrad from Gainesville, Georgia who spoke with such a strong southern accent Finn often had to strain to understand what the hell he was saying. For some reason, Whitney disliked Paul, calling him a "hillbilly hick". Still, Paul was good fun and he and Finn had attended several sporting events together. Paul was a fanatical supporter and a fountain of knowledge about every single detail one would ever need to know about a variety of sports. However, he'd never actually played any.

Finn, on the other hand, was pretty sure he

could swing a bat but he didn't even know what softball was. He had a vague idea of baseball but had never even seen a game.

His colleagues tried to explain. "It's a lot like baseball, only—"

Finn stopped them. "Sorry, lads, the comparison might be helpful if I knew the first thing about baseball, but I don't."

Paul grinned. "That ain't no never mind. I'll give you the Cliff notes version."

Finn had no idea what that was, but it didn't sound at all promising to him.

On the evening of the game, the team assembled early for warm ups. There were just nine of them, enough to fill the outfield, Finn was told. Whitney Campbell was there all decked out in short shorts and a tight tee-shirt, but Morgan Herman was away at the conference.

Finn was a little worried that with Morgan away, he might have to fend off another of Whitney's advances after the game. *With any luck, she'll distract the opposition. Or maybe they'll distract her.*

Finn's team were fielding first and Finn was positioned in right field with instructions to try to catch any ball that came his way or at least get it back to the pitcher as quickly as possible.

"Seems straightforward enough," Finn said to Paul who had been assigned center field.

"Just wait. Unless they have a lefty that pulls, ain't much gonna come your way."

Finn had no fucking clue what that meant.

"On the other hand failure is my destiny. I'll

bet dollars to donuts every ball will be sent in my direction and I undoubtedly will screw up."

Finn tried to encourage him. "Nonsense. You'll be fine."

It turned out Paul was exactly right on both counts. A lot of balls came his way, none of which he caught and those that came along the ground bounced right through his glove. Even after he switched positions with Finn at the third inning, the batters still seemed to find him with great regularity. Finn felt bad for Paul but since they were being slaughtered anyway, he reasoned it didn't matter.

Having been put at the bottom of the roster, Finn hadn't been at bat yet. By the time he was up to bat, there were two out and runners on first and second bases. Whitney was on first having been walked by the pitcher, who seemed to take pity on her. Finn could not expect the same gentle treatment.

When the ball left the pitcher's hand and came his way, Finn paused a moment then swung the bat with all his might. To his and everyone else's surprise, he connected and the ball sailed into the outfield. Finn stood there mesmerized, watching it.

"Run, Finn, run," he finally heard Paul yelling at him. He took off running towards first base.

"Drop the bat, drop the bat," people screamed at him.

Damn. He finally dropped the bat as he got to first base.

"Go to second," Paul yelled, so he took off running again. He reached second base and saw that the ball had not come back in yet so he decided to try for third. When he got halfway there he saw Whitney standing on the base and heard her screaming at him to go back to second. By now the ball was rapidly coming in and it didn't look like he was going to make it back to second base in time.

"Slide, slide," voices chanted at him.

Finn had no clue how to slide but he decided to try it and covered the last eight feet on the ground in a movement that someone remarked later resembled a crab that was completely constipated. He barely made it and stood up triumphantly to see Whitney and everyone else doubled over with laughter.

An opposing team player touched the ball to him.

Surprised, Finn asked, "Am I out?"

"No."

"Then why did you that?"

The other player grinned. "You ever play this game before?"

"What makes you ask that?" Finn replied with a smile.

"Just a wild guess that's all."

"Well, don't tell anyone but it is my first time."

The other player laughed. "Oh hell, boy. I don't need to tell anyone. After your masterful play, there's no one at this game, including my seven-year-old daughter, who doesn't know that."

To no one's surprise, they lost spectacularly.

Later that night in the bar, Finn's team mates took turns at trying to mimic his epic slide. Time and again they asked him to repeat it but he told them honestly since he didn't know how he did it the first time, there was no way he could do it again.

Despite losing, the team declared the game a tremendous success and decided that Finn should play with them for the rest of the season. He politely declined this generous offer.

Later, as he feared, a very drunk Whitney made a serious effort to get him to sleep with her.

"It's not going to happen, Whitney," he told her as she attempted to drape herself all over him.

"Why not?" She pouted. "Aren't I good enough for you? Or is there some nice Irish lassie waiting at home for you?"

"No, it's not that. It's because there's a nice American lad who you've promised to marry."

"Soooooo, if there was no nice American lad, would you?"

"I don't know for sure, but at least it would be a different conversation."

"Well I guess that puts the ball squarely in my court." She swung a make believe tennis racquet. "Swish. Forty love to Miss Campbell. Game, set and match point." She swung again. "Ace. That's it. That's the game for Miss Campbell." She looked at Finn and winked before saying, "Your loss. See you tomorrow, sucker."

Chapter Eighteen

Tuesday, July 15, 1986
Week Four: Day Two

It was three-thirty in the morning when Finn knocked at Julia's front door. They had a six o'clock flight from Dublin to Zurich where they would catch a connection to Lugano. The plan was to check into the hotel, grab a quick shower and be at the conference by noon. It was going to make for a very long day but neither of them had felt like dealing with the awkwardness of going to Dublin the night before and staying in a hotel. There was enough of that to come and it just seemed so much easier to face it in Switzerland than here at home.

Julia opened the door, yawning and looking adorably sleepy. Finn smiled at her. "Hey."

"How can you be so goddam cheerful in the middle of the night?" She pointed to two large bags standing in the hallway. "Can you give me a hand getting these into your car, please? They're a bit heavy."

"Sure. I've got it." Finn retorted reached for them. "*Jesus Christ almighty.* What the hell have you got in these? We're only going for five days."

"Never you mind. I'm a girl, OK? A girl needs stuff. I wasn't sure what type of shoes I'd need so I brought a few pairs. Are you going to put them in the car or not?"

"How many is a few pairs?"

Julia mumbled something under her breath.

Surely she hadn't said what he thought she did. "How many?"

"Seven."

This time he had no trouble hearing her and he was dumbfounded. "You packed more pairs of shoes than the number of days you're going to be away? Seriously?"

Julia shrugged. "Clearly the importance of having the right shoes is lost on you. But don't let it worry you, you'll learn." He loved the light teasing tone of her voice. "Come on, let's go. We don't want to be late now do we?"

"No, *madam*, we don't. Your carriage awaits."

He helped her into the car, loaded her suitcases into the boot and they were off. She was asleep within ten minutes. Finn kept the radio off as he sped through a series of still asleep towns. Traffic was virtually non-existent at that hour of the morning so he was able to make good time. He glanced over at her as she slept. Even at that hour and with no makeup, she was stunningly beautiful. He sincerely hoped this trip would work out. *It could make us or break us.*

When they reached the airport, Finn tapped her shoulder gently. "Wake up. We're here."

Julia sat up quickly. "Huh, we're here? I must have just dozed off. Sorry."

He grinned. "Yeah, you just dozed off as we pulled away from your house. You slept the whole way, dear. So much for keeping the driver company." At the look of concern on her face he added, "I'm just teasing. I'm glad you were able to rest. Let's get checked in and grab a bite to eat."

The first flight was uneventful and they both dozed through it but the second one, in a little propeller plane, was a completely different story. The flight path took them over the Alps and it seemed to Finn that the plane was skimming along the top of the peaks just a few yards above the highest points. There was a lot of turbulence and the little plane lurched violently for most of the journey. No one could have slept on the flight.

Julia was terrified and dug her nails into his arm with each and every bump. Finn tried to reassure her but he wasn't exactly convinced that it was no big deal and that they were perfectly safe. After a harrowing approach and an extremely bumpy landing, the plane gradually came to a halt.

Julia looked green. "I think I'm going to be sick. We're taking the train back on Sunday. Okay?"

Finn nodded. "Anything you want." He was not unhappy with that plan at all.

Chapter Nineteen

Thursday, July 17, 1986
Week Four: Day Four

They were both very busy for the first two days and they didn't see a whole lot of each other except at mealtimes. The grand finale for the conference was a dinner for all attendees in the ballroom. Finn had been looking forward to it for two reasons. First, he knew it would be fun and second, more importantly, it would mean that the conference was over and he would have Julia to himself for the whole weekend.

Now he waited by the elevator on the ground floor. It was almost half past seven and the dinner was about to start. Julia was supposed to have met him here fifteen minutes earlier so they could grab seats together at a table with some friends. He had taken the precaution of asking them to hold a couple of places for them, but these guys had been drinking for the past few hours and there were no guarantees they would even remember. "Come on Julia," he muttered. "What are you doing?"

The hotel lobby was crowded with people milling around. He turned to scan the crowd in case he had somehow missed her. He looked back just as the elevator door opened and had to practically gasp for air.

Julia smiled as she walked towards him. She was wearing a fitted black dress that stopped just above her knees and showed off her figure in the most stunning way possible. She had put her hair up and her only jewelry was a simple gold necklace. He had never seen anything so amazing in all his life.

"Sorry." She smiled at him. "I couldn't decide which shoes to wear." She actually winked.

He glanced briefly at her feet. She wore a pair of black pumps with heels high enough to accentuate the length and shapeliness of her legs.

"Do I look okay?" She seemed to be enjoying the fact that he was lost for words. She leaned in and whispered, "Close your mouth."

Finn finally managed to collect his thoughts and form words. "You look absolutely fabulous. Beautiful, in fact."

"Thank you, kind sir. Now, can I link your arm as I'm not sure I've quite mastered the art of walking in four inch heels."

She took him by the arm and they walked towards the ballroom. Finn was conscious of the swell of her breast against his arm and the soft, citrusy smell that seemed to come from her hair. He felt all eyes on them as they entered the ballroom. With most people already seated, they were making, in effect, a grand entrance. He suspected most of the men in the room were extremely jealous of him right then. They reached the table, sat down and soon were engaged in lively conversation with the other guests.

Dinner at their table turned out to be quite a raucous affair. Their friends continued to drink at pace and, by the time the speeches came around, had become very vocal, inciting a couple of verbal warnings to pipe down. Finally, the speeches reached a merciful conclusion, after which the guests at the table busied themselves with the task of getting absolutely hammered.

It was clear that theirs was the fun table and people started to drift over, bringing their own chairs to join in. One guy plopped his chair down next to Julia and almost immediately began hitting on her. Finn, who had moved to the opposite end of the table to speak with someone earlier, when the drinking picked up, looked across at her with some concern.

First he thought she was uncomfortable but he could see her relaxing and laughing at whatever her pursuer was saying to her.

"I shouldn't worry about it," a voice behind him said. "It's not like she's going to dump you for him."

Finn turned around and saw an attractive blonde with gentle eyes and a kind smile sitting there. "You never know."

"Oh, I can tell you it will only happen in his dreams. Besides, you're far better looking than him. So don't worry."

"Thank you. That obvious, huh?"

"Just a little, but it's nice to see."

Finn looked back over at Julia, who seemed to be really enjoying herself now. "How can you be so sure?" By the way, I'm Finn. Apologies for the lack of manners."

"I'm Claire. Pleased to meet you, Finn. I know, because there's no way she's going to go anywhere with him tonight."

"And you know this how?"

"Because I'm his fiancée. We're getting married in two weeks."

Finn just stared at her in amazement, not sure what to say.

Claire beat him to it. "Right now, you don't know whether to congratulate me or offer your commiserations. We don't really have control over who we fall in love with so I got that." She pointed towards her fiancé, who was piling on the charm with all his might.

"Well then, a little of both, I guess."

"Oh look." Claire laughed. "The poor bugger struck out. I guess he'll just have to make do with me so tonight. Well it was very nice talking to you, Finn. Look after that gorgeous woman of yours." She got up and walked after the very disappointed fiancé.

Julia caught his eye and mouthed, "Are you done?"

Finn nodded. They both stood up, said their goodbyes and left. Julia held onto him again for balance.

"He was such a creep. At first, I thought it was just a bit of harmless flirting but then he became very explicit so it was time for him to go."

"Want me to sort him out?" Finn said in mock menace.

Julia looked at him in horror but then punched his arm when she saw he was joking. "Asshole." Then her eyes twinkled and she added, "But thanks for the offer."

When they reached the lobby she looked up at him. "Right. I'm off to bed. Busy day tomorrow. Are you still up for the drive around the lake to Chamonix?"

"I am. Are you still up for giving skiing a try?"

"I still think it's a little nutters since neither of us have ever done it, but yes, I'm up for it."

"Excellent. When do you want to leave?"

"I'll meet you here for breakfast at nine and we can leave after that."

Finn nodded and then unexpectedly, she leaned in and kissed him softly on the mouth. She stepped back and smiled. "I've wanted to do that all day. Now off with you." But she was the one who turned to leave.

He watched her walk away, still feeling the sensation of her lips on his. He headed to the bar. After that, he needed a nightcap.

Chapter Twenty

Friday, July 18, 1986
Week Four: Day Five

Finn and Julia set out in the rental car immediately after breakfast. It was a bright, cloudless day and the air was warm and dry. They planned to drive around the circumference of the lake, then head up into the Alps. Finn drove carefully, trying to get used to doing so on the other side of the road while changing gears with his right hand instead of his left. Roundabouts were the biggest challenge as his natural tendency was to turn left instead of right once he reached the ramp.

Julia sat back, opened the window and took in the stunning scenery. "It sure is pretty. Hard to beat some of these views."

"Would you like some music to add to the experience? I brought along a couple of my favorite tapes."

"Wow," said Julia in mock surprise, "I'm really impressed. A man who actually thinks ahead. What have you got?"

"Only my top two albums of all time. Leonard Cohen's Greatest Hits and Dire Straits' Making Movies."

Julia groaned. "Those are the choices? I retract my earlier comments. I'm not so impressed after all."

"Don't be like that. Give it a try. You'll love it.

Trust me. Which one do you want first? Note. I said 'first' because you're getting both of them."

"Such a tough decision." Julia rolled her eyes. "I can be bored to tears or bored to tears. You pick. It's your music, after all."

"As you wish, my dear." Finn inserted the Leonard Cohen tape into the deck. "Prepare to be amazed."

After her initial reaction to the starkness of the music and the tonality of Leonard's voice, to her great surprise, Julia admitted to really enjoying the album.

"The lyrics are...well, I can relate."

That didn't surprise Finn. It was hard not to feel the deep emotions in Leonard's mournful lyrics of lost loves, lost lives and the awful pain that living sometimes brings.

"Play that verse again," she asked. "I want to hear those lines once more."

Finn rewound the tape a little and Leonard Cohen's words filled the car. He was singing *Suzanne*.

"This was the very first Leonard Cohen song I ever heard and I was instantly smitten."

"I can see why."

"I read that he was tricked into signing away the rights to this song. He said, probably tongue in cheek, that, 'It would be wrong to write this song and get rich from it too.'"

"You're kidding."

"No. The article said one of the greatest indignities he ever suffered was when he was on a boat in Greece and Judy's rendition of the song was played on the radio much to the delight of the other passengers."

"That's so sad, to think that you could so easily lose something so beautiful and so precious."

Finn looked over at her. Her eyes had teared up a little.

She turned to look at him. "Jesus, that could have been written about us. It's eerie. I take my comment back yet again. You really do plan ahead, don't you?"

Finn just smiled to himself and said nothing.

They stopped for lunch at a little restaurant at the far end of the lake. The view was absolutely breathtaking and though it had turned a little chilly, they sat outside. Julia drank two glasses of wine while Finn had to content himself with soda.

"I should feel guilty, I know," she said, "but to be perfectly honest, I don't."

"Oh well, at least you're honest. I feel so much better now."

After lunch, they drove for another couple of hours up into the Alps. It was much colder now and the air was thinner. They came across a little ski resort and decided to try it out for a laugh.

During the summer months, the resort stayed open by using a mixture of natural and artificial snow. Experienced skiers generally stayed away but it was perfect for novices such as Finn and Julia. Twenty minutes later, they were all decked out in proper ski gear and trying to understand what the instructor was saying to them.

"This should be interesting," Finn muttered. "Let's hope there are no broken bones afterwards."

The instructor led them out to the beginner slope and told them not to ski anywhere else other than in this area.

"No worries about that, mate. This is adventurous enough for me."

Slowly and gingerly they inched their way forward, following the instructor's words as best they could. It was hard going but Finn could see that Julia was enjoying herself.

"Come on slow poke," she yelled back at him, "there are four year olds out here moving faster than you."

"I wasn't aware it was a race."

She laughed. "It's not, but the idea is to keep moving, not stand still." She turned and headed back towards him, showing off her mastery of the poles. When she was within three feet of him, she lost her balance and ploughed directly into Finn, knocking him flat and landing right on top of him.

Finn laughed out loud. "That's what you get for showing off." He then became aware of the fact that she was lying on top of him and looking directly into his eyes. They held each other's gaze for what seemed like ages before kissing. This time, the kiss was deeper and more passionate than last night's.

"I could get used to this," Finn whispered when she finally broke the kiss.

"Me too, and that's what scares me." She got off him and picked up her ski poles. "What do you think? Enough of the piste for today?"

"Absolutely. My thighs are killing me."

They headed back to the hotel listening to Dire Straits once and Leonard Cohen twice more. Julia was by now a committed fan and Finn promised to lend her more of his albums. It was late by the time they reached the hotel. Neither of them was hungry and they decided to call it a night. Tomorrow they were going to check out of the hotel early, then drive into Italy and see how far they got before stopping for the night.

Julia hugged him quickly. "Thanks for a lovely day. Good night."

"Thank you too. See you in the morning."

Chapter Twenty-One

December, 1983
Edgarville, Kentucky

After the night of the softball game, Whitney stopped propositioning Finn. She was still as friendly as ever towards him and he began to relax more in her company. Perhaps this is why he began to notice odd changes in her. On several occasions she appeared to grimace in pain when she lifted something or when she stretched.

He asked her about it a couple of times. Each time she replied that she was fine but her eyes and overall demeanor gave the impression that she was hiding something.

He asked Paul about it one night when they were sitting in the bar enjoying a beer.

"I think she's playing you, man."

"You don't think Morgan could be hurting her do you?"

Paul shook his head. "No way in hell, he's doing that to the Snow Queen." This was Paul's favorite nickname for Whitney. "That chick has ice water in her veins and she could chew you up and spit you out without moving her mouth."

Finn wasn't sure what to think. Morgan certainly never gave the impression that he could be violent towards Whitney. But there was definitely something going on with her. Even her appearance had changed recently. Her clothes were more demure and conservative, much to the ongoing disappointment of the men in the chemistry department. Still, there was little he could do. She didn't display any bruises or cuts and she reassured him she was fine each time he asked. He would just have to keep an eye on her.

The opportunity to do just that came when he was halfway through his fourth month. Whitney arrived in the lab one morning, slapped a ticket on his desk and asked Finn if he'd like to go to a Bruce Springsteen concert with her.

Finn was a huge Springsteen fan and he'd told Whitney he hoped to see him live before his time at KenTech was up.

"Wow. When? Where?" He was completely taken aback.

"Next Saturday in Lexington. I managed to snag two tickets. We'll drive there, stay overnight and head back the next day."

So there it was. Finn's excitement faded rapidly. An overnight trip for just the two of them. If that was the price of admission it was beyond his budget.

Whitney clearly read the change in his demeanor. "It's not what you think, honest. First, Morgan is cool with this. That's Mother's Day weekend and his Beaver Cleaver family will all assemble to pay homage to the matriarch. Second, I know you love Springsteen and this is your only opportunity to see him live. Third, you can strap on your chastity belt. I promise there'll be no hanky-panky. Come on, what do you say? I know you want to." She waved the ticket in front of his face, teasing him.

Finn was torn. He definitely wanted to go but he knew, despite Whitney's protestations to the contrary, this was a trip that was laden with minefields. He made a decision.

"I'll go on one condition."

"Which is?" Whitney asked, a little annoyed.

"My condition is that I ask Morgan if he really is okay with this. If he is as you say, then thank you, I'll be delighted to go. If he's even the slightest bit uncomfortable, then I'm going to have to turn down this very kind offer."

To his surprise, she smiled broadly and said, "Then it's a date. You go ask Morgan. I'll be here with the tickets."

"Okay. I'll go ask him."

Again Finn was surprised. While Morgan wasn't exactly dancing a jig for joy at the prospect of his totally hot fiancée overnighting alone with the handsome Irish scientist, he seem totally relaxed about the whole thing.

"To be honest, I'm glad you're going with her. These concerts can get quite messy and I'd be worried if she was there with just one of her girlfriends. She's not exactly invisible as you know and attention does follow her around. I'll be a lot more comfortable knowing you're there to look after her."

If there was any lack of sincerity behind those surprising words, Finn could not discern it. Morgan had looked him calmly in the eye, shook his hand and told him to have a good time.

Finn left Morgan's lab and headed back to his

own, completely perplexed. He wasn't sure he'd be as copacetic about this as Morgan was, but despite Finn's misgivings, his condition had been met and he was definitely looking forward to seeing Springsteen. He would have to remain vigilant but he could handle that.

"Well?" Whitney asked when he returned to the lab.

"It looks like we're on."

"See, I told you so. Now, let's make plans for our road trip."

Chapter Twenty-Two

Saturday, July 19, 1986
Week Four: Day Six

"Do we actually have any sort of a plan here?" Finn asked as they set off that morning.

"Oh yes, we do. I have it all mapped out. See, it's not just you who thinks ahead. You drive and I'll give you instructions. That's the way it should be anyway."

Finn pretended to groan in frustration. "I can already tell this is going to be a fun day."

Which is exactly what the day turned out to be. Julia had put a lot of effort into the trip and had mapped out a route that took them to several small villages and towns where they stopped to look at beautiful old churches, castles, monuments and other works of art as well as just the local scenery itself. Finn was very impressed with the thoroughness of her preparation and ended up being fascinated by many of the intriguing sites she took them to.

They sat outside for lunch in a tiny little village, which seemed to have only one street and one restaurant. The views, however, were spectacular. Mountains in one direction and a deep valley in another. Finn couldn't be happier as he sipped a double espresso whilst Julia liberally sampled the local wine.

"Magnifico," she proclaimed happily.

"You know, this whole driving thing is getting rather old," Finn grumbled just to annoy her a little.

Julia, unfazed, smiled brightly at him and sampled yet another Chianti. "Those are the breaks, my friend. Don't worry, I'm sure there'll be plenty of wine left for you after we stop for the night."

"Speaking of which, do you have any idea where we'll stop?"

Julia shook her head. "None at all."

Finn knew that wasn't true. He was certain she had every detail planned but he left it at that anyway.

After lunch, and yet another Chianti for Julia, they set off again. It was after three in the afternoon and the weather was absolutely perfect.

"Don't you fall asleep now after all that wine," Finn warned her.

"I won't," she promised but did anyway within twenty minutes.

Finn pulled over, gently prised the map from her hands and studied the route she had mapped out. As best he could figure, she had planned for them to spend the night in a little town called Chiavenna, which would leave them with a three hour drive back to Lugano tomorrow. They had a two o'clock connection to Zurich and a four o'clock onward flight to Dublin which should put them back in Lissadown before eight that evening.

Julia slept the remainder of the two hour journey to Chiavenna and Finn only woke her up as they drove down the tree-lined main street. He gently shook her shoulder. "Wakey, wakey sleepy head."

She awoke with a start, looked at her watch then out the window. "Oh my God, look at the time. You let me sleep the whole way. You are a good man, Finn Lane."

"Don't I know it. Did you research any hotels or is it just pot luck?"

"I didn't get that far, but I'm sure there are several to choose from."

"Well there's one right there." Finn pointed in the direction of a small, compact building with a neon hotel sign running down the outer wall. "Let's try it."

They parked the car and walked to the hotel. The main street of Chiavenna was extremely picturesque and the town itself had a very sleepy feel to it.

Julia glanced around. "I'm not sure this is the liveliest town in all of Italy."

"But we live in Lissadown, so who are we to judge?"

Julia laughed and readjusted her grip on her suitcase.

"Here, let me carry that for you." Finn took the bag from her then pretended to drop under the weight of her suitcase.

She arched a brow at him. "It's still not funny and it's never going to be."

He chuckled. "It is to me."

They climbed four steps and walked through the revolving door into the lobby of the hotel. There was a fire burning in the corner, lots of old pictures on the walls and the overall effect was warm and welcoming.

"I like it so far," Finn whispered.

He walked over to the reception desk, behind which stood a middle-aged man. "Do you speak English, please?"

The man nodded.

"Good, then we'd like—"

"One double room, please," Julia finished his sentence.

He spun around in amazement to look at her but she ignored him and repeated her request. "One double room, please."

Finn turned back to the desk clerk, who now had a big smile plastered across his face. "I think the lady has a better idea, yes?" He laughed delightedly.

"I guess so." Finn's mind raced at this wholly unexpected development.

They took the key, left the still smiling clerk and took the elevator to their room on the third floor in silence. The room itself was clean and airy with a balcony that overlooked the main street along with a big double bed in the center.

Julia walked over to Finn and took his face in her hands. "Look, I hope I haven't done something wrong here. Nothing is going to happen tonight, you need to understand that upfront. But I've had such a lovely time that I thought it would be nice to spend the night with you and have you hold me. I'm sorry if that's selfish and I'll understand if you want to get your own room."

She looked at him worriedly as Finn processed her words. He smiled reassuringly at her. "That works. Honest. I've had a great time too and, yes,

I'd like nothing better than to hold you tonight."

"You sure? For real?"

"For real."

"Okay." The relief in her voice was palpable. "Now you get yourself down to the bar and have a couple of drinks, I'm going to take a nap. I'm really tired."

Finn looked at her askance. "You're not serious."

She laughed. "No I'm not. It was a joke. I want to take a shower and get changed. I'll join you in the bar later and we can go for dinner afterwards. You deserve a drink on so many levels, so scoot."

When he passed by the reception desk on the way to the bar, the clerk winked at him and gave him the thumbs up sign. "You're enjoying this way too much," Finn grumbled.

The bar was quaint and quiet. It had dark wood paneling all round, comfortable, well-worn leather seats and a great selection of Italian wines. After a little bit of a challenging discussion with the waiter, whose English was as bad as Finn's Italian, he decided on a glass of Brunello Montalcino. He wasn't familiar with it but the waiter said "*bella*" enough times to convince him.

Finn sat at a table in the corner and slowly sipped the wine, which was indeed very pleasant. His thoughts wandered to the weekend so far and Julia's insistence on sharing a room tonight. *Steady on,* he warned himself, *don't mess this up by being stupid.* He knew he could totally blow his whole relationship with Julia if he made an unwelcome move tonight.

At the back of his mind, he wondered if this was some kind of a test but he knew she wasn't that devious. He had no sooner finished his glass when the waiter arrived at the table with a refill.

This is the life. He sat back and relaxed. He was feeling good. His body was almost completely healed and he was going back to his usual workout routine on Monday. After about fifteen minutes, Julia appeared at the door of the bar looking radiant. She was wearing a long, purplish sundress that reached her ankles with flip flops on her feet. Her dark hair nestled gently on her shoulder.

Finn stood up to greet her. "You look very nice. Now I see the benefits of bringing your whole wardrobe with you. What can I get you? I'm drinking Brunello, which is very nice but since you've already had lots of wine, maybe a coffee."

"First, thank you for the compliment. Second, fuck you for your comment about my luggage and third, yes, I'd love a Brunello. The Chianti was hours ago." All this was said with a sweet, innocent smile on her face. After the waiter brought her drink, they sat there, relaxed and content. Over the last few days, it became clear that, happy in each other's company, neither of them needed constant conversation.

After one more glass of wine each, they asked for a recommendation for dinner. Their choices were apparently limited but the smiling clerk assured them that the restaurant at the bottom of the street was top class.

"His smug smirk is beginning to annoy me," Finn muttered under his breath as they walked out of the hotel.

"Oh relax, you grouchy old goat." She slipped her hand into his. "He's just having fun. You have to admit, it was funny and that look on your face, priceless. Totally priceless."

"Well I'm glad I'm such a source of amusement to you all." He wanted to sound affronted, but as thrilled as he was that she'd taken his hand, he just couldn't pull it off.

They wandered slowly down the old street towards the restaurant, admiring buildings and trees along the way. It was a warm night. Julia had brought a cardigan but Finn felt comfortable in his shirt sleeves. The restaurant looked like it was several hundred years old. The interior was sparsely furnished and the lighting dim.

"Nice ambience," he whispered to Julia, who ignored him completely. That's another thing he'd noticed about her; she only responded when she felt like it.

It was cooler inside and Julia put on her cardigan once they were seated.

They then encountered a major challenge in that the menus were all in Italian and none of the staff spoke any English. Eventually, they figured out that the staff would select their meal for them. Finn asked for a bottle of Brunello, feeling confident that the wine would at least be good.

The waiter-tut tutted and shook his head while spewing out a long stream of Italian. Clearly they intended to select the wine too. Finn and Julia both shrugged. "Ah well," said Finn, "might as well be hung for a sheep as for a lamb. Do your worst."

After a few minutes, the waiter brought a large plate of antipasti and some bruschetta. This was paired with a very light red, almost rose wine. Their second course was a pasta dish with wild mushrooms that was absolutely delicious. This time the wine chosen for them was a heavier, drier wine that complimented the dish perfectly. The fish course consisted of branzino lightly grilled in olive oil and served with the freshest tasting tomatoes either of them had ever encountered. For this dish, the waiter chose a crisp white which also worked perfectly.

Just when Finn thought he couldn't possibly eat another bite, the waiter appeared with large portions of homemade tiramisu. "No way." Finn started to wave him off. "I'm so full that I won't be able to eat until Monday."

Julia's eyes twinkled mischievously. "If you share it with me, I'll kiss you when we get outside."

"Shame on you," Finn responded in mock horror, "trying to bribe like that. Unconscionable."

Julia laughed. "I take it that's a 'yes'?"

"Is the bear a Catholic? Where's my spoon."

After dinner, they wandered over to the restaurant bar where the shelves were stocked with rows and rows of all sorts of weird and wonderful alcoholic drinks. They sampled several grappas and sambucas and neither of them were perfectly sober when they left.

Outside, Julia drew him towards her and kissed him passionately. "I hate to be a buzz kill but remember this is as far as it goes. I hope you don't think I'm leading you on."

"No," agreed Finn, "we have a deal."

Thankfully, there was a new clerk behind the reception desk when they asked for their key. Once they reached the room, Julia went to the bathroom to change and brush her teeth. At that moment Finn realized something and shouted to Julia through the door. "Uh...Julia. I don't have pajamas. I normally sleep in my jocks."

"Then that will have to do. Unless you want to borrow a pair of mine."

"Funny girl."

Just then, the bathroom door opened and Julia, wearing a long tee-shirt and pajama bottoms, stood there. She shrugged, a little apologetically. "Not very sexy but under the circumstances, probably for the best."

She started to edge past him towards the bed, but he stopped her. "Julia, you are beautiful no matter what you wear."

She blushed, flustered but clearly pleased by his words. "Go on. The bathroom's yours now."

By the time Finn came out of the bathroom, the room was in darkness. He climbed into bed wanting to pull her into his arms but knowing he had to leave it in her hands.

Almost instantly she scooted towards him, then turned her back once she was lying against him. "Can you put your arm around me, please?"

Finn did and felt the warmth of her body snug against him.

A few hours later, he woke up and he was completely hard. Julia was still pressed against him and he could feel her backside tight against his erection. He lay there for a moment unsure what to do when he felt Julia's hand reach into his underwear. She took his length in her hand and began to slowly stroke him up and down. She never moved her body, nor made a sound. She gave no sign that she was even awake but she kept stroking him with a slow, steady rhythm until Finn could feel the desire to come building up in him. Finally, he could take it no more. He moaned loudly as he came.

"Shh," whispered Julia, "you'll disturb the neighbors." This was all she said. Then she took his hand and placed it on her breast. They fell fast asleep almost immediately.

Chapter Twenty-Three

Sunday, July 20, 1986
Week Four: Day Seven

Julia was already in the shower when Finn woke up on Sunday morning. He lay there, hands behind his head, trying to figure what the hell was going on. *It's like being on a frigging roller coaster.* On the one hand, Julia was adamant that she wasn't ready for a relationship nor was she prepared to be sexually intimate with him. On the other hand, she flirted with him madly and just last night had given him one of the most intense sexual experiences of his life.

She's treading unknown waters, he reminded himself. She had survived a heinous attack and was trying to find her way too. Still, they had to talk about this.

But not today. He would wait a week so as not to spoil what had been a truly great time.

Julia came out of the bathroom fully dressed. "Sorry, did I wake you?"

"Not at all."

"Okay. Good. I'm going to go for a walk and how about we meet downstairs for breakfast afterwards? How long do you need? No rush."

Finn looked at her, considered saying something then simply replied, "Half an hour okay?"

Julia nodded. "See you then."

By the time they finished breakfast, the awkwardness Finn had noticed in the room earlier had completely dissipated.

Julia herself raised the issue. "Look, I know you think I'm giving you mixed signals but it's not meant to be like that, I promise. I'm all messed up after what happened and scared shitless about being naked with a man or the prospect of having sex. But I really do like you, more than that actually. And last night, it just felt so good to be in your arms, I wanted to give you something in return. I'm sorry if I complicated anything or confused you or hurt you."

Finn leaned across the table and kissed her forehead. "Say no more. This has been a very special time and last night made it even more so. I know how difficult it must have been for you and I love you all the more for it."

She smiled across at him. "That's just it. It wasn't difficult at all. I thought it would be, but it wasn't. It was my choice. My gift to give. It's different. Does that make sense?"

He nodded.

"At times, I think I'm so lucky that you entered my life and that makes me terrified because I've always thought that I'm a truly unlucky person."

Finn took her hand and stroked it gently. "Let's hit the road." His voice was tight with emotion.

Ten hours later, he dropped her off at her home in Lissadown.

She kissed him softly. "Thank you so much. I will never, ever forget this weekend."

I won't either, my beautiful girl. Finn watched

her enter her house.

~ * ~

Julia went inside, left her bags in the hall and went straight to the kitchen where she opened a bottle of wine. She took a big gulp out of the glass and then another. Her head was spinning and she felt like she was no longer in control of her thoughts and her emotions. She knew she was falling in love, or to be more accurate, was already in love with Finn.

She had just spent several days without having to look over her shoulder or be worried that she could be attacked at any moment. It had been such a carefree feeling. Finn had been such great company. He made her laugh, he made her feel safe and on top of that he made her feel beautiful.

In her eyes, she was broken and ugly yet here was this gorgeous man who looked at her in a way that made her feel like she was Miss Universe. "I don't get it," she said out loud before taking another big gulp of wine. "He could have any woman he wanted yet here he is with a half-person who has very little to give him."

She worried that he would get fed up with her. She was traumatized by the prospect of being naked with him or, worse still, having sex with him, as she feared the images of what those bastards did to her would play in her mind then.

On the other hand, if she gave herself freely to him, he would no doubt be completely turned off by the sight of her body with its ugly scars and burn marks. "Hobson's fucking choice." She laughed bitterly. "Damned if you do and damned if you don't. As I always say, 'Girl, you are one unlucky bitch.'"

She went to bed angry at herself for having completely destroyed the high that she had been on before she walked in the door.

Chapter Twenty-Four

Thursday, July 24, 1986
Week Five: Day Four

The week had passed by in a blur. Finn could scarcely believe it was Thursday evening already. He had restarted his daily workout routine as planned and his body felt good. Sore but good. His boss had tried his level best not to smirk when Finn handed in his report on the conference. Rumors were abounding around Roan that Finn and Julia were an item and that it was serious. His boss was clearly well aware of this and, it would seem, not a little chuffed about it.

The workplace atmosphere had improved dramatically for Julia, and for most other employees as well, and the whole tone of the place was vastly different since the big showdown a few weeks back. Lissadown was still a very dangerous place and nobody assumed that everything was roses. There were, however, growing signs that the police were gradually retaking control and that there was at least some hope for a better future.

Finn was looking forward to tomorrow night as he and Julia had made reservations for dinner at Le Chapeau restaurant, which was by far the best in Lissadown.

~ * ~

Although Julia was also looking forward to her

date with Finn, she could feel a growing sense of anxiety with every passing day as she grew closer and closer to him. There was no doubt in her mind now that she had fallen in love with the extremely handsome Dr. Finn Lane. The problem was what to do with this love and where to let it take her.

To her own great surprise, she found herself wanting to be physically intimate with Finn. She had been certain for so long that this would never be the case for her again and now everything had been upended. That night in Italy had been a breakthrough. She had been in control. She had made the choice to give of herself, no matter how small that step was, and it hadn't been traumatic. What had happened to her was the last thing on her mind at that moment. Her one desire had been to make him feel good, and doing so gave her pleasure.

Julia's far bigger fear was having to expose her body to Finn. Doing that would be taking a huge risk and she wasn't sure if she was ready for that. *Have him in my life at arms' length, or show him what I truly am and watch him run the other way? Now there's a choice any girl would love to make, right?*

Tomorrow night was shaping up to be the biggest night of their relationship and it could all be over by Saturday morning. "Julia dearest," she said out loud, "You've got to roll the dice sometime."

Chapter Twenty-Five

December, 1983
Lexington, Kentucky

Whitney arrived at his door promptly at ten on the morning of the concert. Lexington was a six hour drive from Edgarville. The plan was to check in at the motel where they had reserved two rooms, drop off their bags and car then take a cab to the stadium where the concert was to be held. Finn was still not without misgivings about the trip and his heart sank when he saw what Whitney was wearing.

The conservative, demure look she had been fostering for the past several weeks was gone and she had fully reverted to her previous sexy Whitney style. Her barely there micro-miniskirt and tight tee-shirt, under which there wasn't a bra, seemed to Finn like a statement of intent. His fears were further compounded when she bent over to pick up his backpack and her skirt rode up, revealing a tiny, white lace thong that barely covered anything.

Somehow sensing where his attention might be, she stayed in that position a few seconds longer than necessary before asking, "Enjoying the view?"

Finn coughed and adopted a warning tone. "Whitney, cut that out."

"Cut what out? I'm not the one looking up someone's skirt." She straightened up and turned to face him, a big grin plastered on her face. "So, did you pack your chastity belt?"

"I most certainly did, and double locks."

"That's good. You'll need it. The women at Springsteen concerts can get very raunchy."

This interchange relaxed the tension that had been building. She punched him in the arm. "Come on you *gobshite*, let's go."

Finn had taught her a few Irish words and Irish sayings. She was particularly enamored with "gobshite" and the fact that saying "I will, yeah," in response to a request to do something actually meant, "No, I won't."

"What a great way to look at life." She had laughed when she learned that one. "Saying 'yes' but meaning 'no'. Hard to beat that."

Finn had looked at her and with great solemnity intoned, "Medieval Irish people moved in the direct antithesis of yes and no."

"What the fuck does that mean?"

"Beats the shit out of me but my high school math teacher said it all the time."

"You people are nuts. Certifiably nuts."

Now, they hopped in Whitney's car and hit the road. They had planned to share driving responsibilities even though Whitney was a tad dubious about this since Finn's experience of driving on "the wrong side of the road" was very limited.

The trip to Lexington was good fun or "good craic" as Whitney pronounced in her best Irish accent. For all her faults, Finn had to admit that Whitney really was great company and he genuinely enjoyed being with her.

The motel that she had booked was a dive but it

was conveniently close to the stadium and they had rooms available.

"Well it sure as shit isn't The Plaza," Whitney declared as they sat in the parking lot staring at the dingy, rundown buildings that looked like they hadn't been painted in fifty years. "I'm not sure I want to see the inside. You go take a look."

Finn walked to reception, paid upfront for the rooms and slowly opened the door to one with the key he had been given. The room was small and sparsely furnished but it seemed clean and was free of any offensive odors. He turned and gave a thumbs up to the anxiously waiting Whitney.

"If you're messing with me, you'll be sorry," she said crossly as she tentatively peered into the room. "Well, okay then, I guess it won't kill us. I'm not getting under those bed covers though and I suggest you don't either."

Finn laughed. He was quite relieved himself but he was nowhere near as squeamish as she apparently was.

The concert was absolutely incredible. Springsteen and the E Street Band put on a show that lasted three and a half hours and was full of energy and passion. Even though they played for such a long time, no one in the audience wanted the concert to end. Whitney had snagged great tickets and they were down on the field right in front of the stage. It was totally mobbed there but the crowd was good-humored and the sweet smell of pot hung low in the air.

There were so many brilliant moments that Finn lost count, but the absolute highlight of the night for him was when Bruce sang a slowed down version of *Thunder Road* accompanied only by a piano and mouth organ. It was magical and the audience was so totally transfixed that there wasn't a sound anywhere. During the song, Whitney took his arm, draped it across her chest and pressed herself to him. For once, Finn didn't object, believing that she was just as much caught up in the moment as everyone else. When the song ended, she looked up at him, her eyes shining with tears, and said, "Now that's a moment that I'll remember for the rest of my life."

"Me too." He gave her a big hug.

After the concert, they went for a night cap in a dingy bar across the street from the motel where they relived the whole experience.

"I'm so glad I got to share this with you," Finn said to her. "And I'm equally glad Morgan was so cool about it."

"Why wouldn't he be?" Whitney replied with an edge in her voice. "He trusts you."

There was an obvious implication in that statement but Finn had had such a good night that he didn't want to open any can of worms by pursuing it. Instead, he merely replied, "Honestly, I can't thank you enough. I'll always remember this day and you every time I hear a Springsteen song."

Whitney smiled brightly. "And every time you wear one of the five Springsteen tee-shirts you bought too, right?"

"Absolutely. Would you like another drink?"

"No thanks. I'm done for the night."

They walked across the road to the motel. Finn

had worried about this moment for the past week.

When they reached the doors of their adjoining rooms, Whitney kissed him softly and briefly on the lips. "Good night Finn. Sleep well. See you in the morning."

Finn stood and watched her enter her room. Before she closed the door, she poked her head out. "Make sure you lock your door. You never know what type of wanton, craven women are roaming the neighborhood." The door closed behind her and he heard her locking it from the inside.

Happily surprised, Finn went to his room and lay on the bed. There was a part of him that cautioned that he wasn't entirely out of the woods yet but he felt like they had passed a big test with flying colors.

The next thing he knew, he was waking to someone banging on his door. Startled, he opened it quickly.

Whitney stood there, smiling brightly. "Rise and shine, sleepyhead. I've got coffee, juice and bagels."

Finn looked around groggily. It was morning. "What time is it?"

"It's after ten. Why don't you take a shower and meet me over at those picnic tables. You look like you could do with one."

After breakfast, they started on the return journey to Edgarville. Finn took first shift driving. He was now convinced that he and Whitney could be friends without any sexual tension between them and he was very glad as she had become an important person to him.

He was so convinced of this that when, after an hour or so, Whitney put her feet up cn the dashboard and her skirt rode up, revealing her underwear, he didn't react. This time she was wearing a black thong that looked so flimsy it seemed like it could fall apart to the touch. Whitney left her skirt there for a moment, so Finn looked at her, then looked between her legs and back at her before stating, with a grin on his face, "It had to have been a man who invented thongs. Whoever he was, he was pure genius and the entire male population on earth owe him a huge debt of gratitude."

Whitney fixed her skirt before replying, "Why dear me, Finn Lane, if I didn't know better I'd think there was a compliment buried deep in that comment."

Finn looked over at her. "I'm sorry. I didn't mean to be so obtuse and force you to have to search so hard for the compliment. That was a great view and that's a compliment."

He felt really good now. He knew for sure that this was just Whitney's playful nature and, even if it was a little edgy, she wasn't hitting on him.

He tried to explain this to a highly skeptical Paul that night after they got back to Edgarville. Paul had been eager to hear how the concert had been and even more eager to hear the gossip and scandal he was convinced Finn would have to share.

"I swear, dude. Nothing happened. Nothing at all."

Paul was initially convinced that Finn was keeping the truth from him but he also knew Finn well enough to know that he wouldn't lie to him.

"So you two are best buds now?

"Buds?"

"Buddies. Pals. Friends.

Finn chuckled. "You could say that."

"Who'da thunk it possible?"

"Yep. Me and the Snow Queen. Best buds."

Chapter Twenty-Six

Friday, July 25, 1986
Week Five: Day Five

Margo Kirk sat in the car park of Roan Pharmaceuticals. It was almost four-forty and she had positioned herself where she could not be seen very easily but where she had a good view of the main door. She knew from her reconnaissance that Finn would leave no later than ten past five. She was determined to confront him so she had driven here with a plan to follow him home. Margo was convinced something major was up. She had become very suspicious when her brother, David, had arrived home one day with Finn's car and some cockeyed story about how they had swapped for a few weeks so that Finn could see how David's handled because he was interested in buying one. "Such total bullshit," she had shouted at David but he refused to give her any more information or even tell her where Finn lived in Lissadown.

Well I'm here now and I'll find it out for myself.

She sat up straight when she saw Finn leave the building with a dark-haired girl by his side. They stopped to chat at the edge of the pavement and even from that distance Margo could see their body language. "What the fuck? Who is she?"

She had to admit that the girl was very pretty and had a gorgeous figure. She was also very familiar. Margo watched as their hands touched briefly when they said goodbye. At that moment, she knew who the girl was and her plans changed. Instead of following Finn she would tail the girl home. "Mother was right. We do know someone working there. Now, how about that?"

Margo waited for a few minutes after Julia had gotten home then walked from her car to the front door and rang the bell. When Julia opened the door, Margo stuck out her hand and smiled brightly. "Hi Julia. I'm Margo. I was a friend of your brother's."

Julia looked at her in shock for a moment before saying, "Oh, please come in."

Margo smiled as she stepped through the door. *Bingo. I was right.*

They went into the living room. "Can I get you something to drink?" Julia asked.

"Alcohol. The stronger the better for both of us. I have a story for you that will come as a big shock."

~ * ~

At a little past seven, Finn parked his car on Julia's street and started to walk towards her house. He was really looking forward to dinner. He had heard great reviews about this restaurant and the prospect of a long, leisurely dinner with Julia was just the ticket for a Friday night. They had both been very busy all week and hadn't spent much time together but he could tell that she was as much in love with him as he was with her.

Then he saw something that startled him out of his reverie. But it couldn't be Margo Kirk's car. She had no reason to be here. When he got closer and saw the Cork registration along with the collection of stuffed animals Margo kept in the rear window, he knew it was hers.

What the hell? Then it dawned on him. He bent over as if he had been sucker-punched. *Oh, Jesus no*, he prayed. *No, no, no.* He never imagined she'd do this and yet here she was. Margo could wreak unbridled havoc. He could handle Margo, but the damage she could cause Julia terrified him. He nearly ran to Julia's door almost in a daze and was not in the least surprised when it was Margo who opened it after he had rang the bell.

"Finn, how are you? Come right in. We've been expecting you."

Finn pushed past her and strode to the living room. There he found Julia, curled up in a ball, sobbing uncontrollably.

"Is it true?" The anguish in her voice tore at his heart. "Please Finn. I have to know. Is it true? You were a friend of my brother's and he asked you to help him because he was afraid for his life but you wouldn't. You went off on holiday when you knew his life was in danger and when you came back, he was dead. Is that true?" Her voice rose and she got up from the couch.

"*Tell me you bastard!* Was that the plan? Rescue the sister because you felt guilty for not helping the brother?" She trembled with rage. "Or did you just want to fuck me over too like everyone else? At least they didn't pretend to like or make me feel like I was actually someone they cared about. What you've done to me is far worse than anything those bastards who raped me did. Eventually, I'll get over how they hurt me. But this…I don't know how I can ever recover from this."

By now she was uncontrollable, her eyes were wild with anger and her face smeared with a mixture of tears and sweat.

Finn stood there rooted to the spot. He didn't know what to say, what words would make a difference to her now.

Even Margo seemed shocked into numbness. She had started this but it appeared as if she was starting to feel pangs of guilt, such was the pain Julia was suffering.

"It wasn't like that. What she told you isn't true."

"Were you a friend of my brother's?" Julia almost spat at him.

"Yes," Finn said quietly.

"Did he ask you for help?"

Finn just nodded again, his heart aching.

"*And you didn't help him?*" she screamed.

"Please, listen Julia, it wasn't like that. It's not that simple."

"Yes or fucking no. that's all I want you to say right now. Yes or no."

"No. I didn't." Finn shook his head. "I didn't."

~ * ~

Julia sat back suddenly as if the enormity of his words had knocked her over. She had heard them from Margo but hearing it directly from Finn was a mortal blow. Just two hours ago, she was in love with him and had been thinking about a future for the two of them together. Now, after all she had suffered in the past, she had just been dealt the worst blow she could ever have imagined. The man she loved was a coward, a liar and a dirty rotten cheat.

She couldn't take it anymore. She was completely enraged. "Get the fuck out of my house, and get the fuck out of my life. Don't look at me, don't talk to me. Nothing. Ever again. Do you understand me?"

"Julia—"

"And take that fucking whore with you. She told about the great sex you've had with her so why don't you go fuck her tonight—or better yet, go fuck yourself." She stopped. "But answer me honestly. For once just tell me the truth. Was all this planned? Did you come to Lissadown because of me? Hadn't you caused our family enough pain that you needed to ruin my life also? What kind of a person are you?"

"Julia," Finn pleaded, "please listen to me. I would never do anything to hurt you. I admit I made some mistakes but I never set out to fall in love with you. That just happened all by itself. I've loved you since you were ten when I saved you from those teenagers."

Both Julia and Margo looked at Finn in amazement.

Julia got there first. "That was you?"

"That was her?" Echoed Margo. "Well that explains a lot."

Julia was completely taken aback by this latest revelation. She looked at Finn then at Margo then back at Finn, almost uncomprehendingly. "I just don't fucking believe this. Can this night get any worse?"

She had to regain control. She rallied herself, walked to the door and in an eerily calm voice said, "Out now. Both of you."

"Julia—"

"Just get the fuck out and leave me alone."

She slammed the door behind them.

~ * ~

He should have told her. He should have told her on his first day at Roan. It would have ruined any chance he had at earning her heart, but it wouldn't have destroyed her as this had. The truth was, he should have let Brian tell her years ago. He should have risked it then and perhaps none of this would have happened.

Once outside, Finn turned to Margo and growled, "You dirty fucking cunt. How could you? You know that's not what happened."

"I don't know, Finn. For what it's worth, I'm sorry, I wasn't thinking straight. I was jealous and I was hurt. I'm sorry."

"You haven't the first fucking clue about the damage you've done."

"I think I do. I'm sorry."

"It doesn't matter now, does it? Go home, Margo. There's been too much said tonight that will be regretted in the future. Let's not add to it."

He walked to his car, leaving her standing there. He drove home in a daze and once there, he opened a bottle of whiskey and drank until he passed out.

~ * ~

Julia sank to the floor and sobbed. What she had just experienced was possibly even worse than what had happened to her the night she had been attacked. Her whole world was shattered. From the moment Margo had stood in her doorway to when she had kicked her and Finn out, Julia felt as if she had moved outside of her body and was watching the scene unfold in her living room from a distance. The whole thing was surreal. The man who she had fallen in love with and who had given her a reason to want to live again when she had thought there never again would be one, had turned out be a phony. He had been a friend of her brother's but had not helped him when he could have. Seeming he had only came to Lissadown to be with her out of guilt. How could anyone be so cruel, especially to a person who had lost what she had and suffered so much? It was inhumane.

This was the last straw. It was over. She was going to leave Lissadown. Tomorrow she would hand in her notice and in two weeks she would be out of here for good. She was sorry now that she hadn't resigned weeks ago as she had originally planned. She could have saved herself all this pain and heartache.

"Fuck you, Finn Lane," she cried out in anguish. "I was doing all right. I was getting by. Now, I'll never get by again."

Chapter Twenty-Seven

January, 1985
Eighteen Months Earlier
Shannon Airport

Finn and David sat in the bar at Shannon Airport. They were waiting to catch a flight to New York from where they had a connection to Miami. After a four hour layover in Miami, it was then on to Rio. Finn had been selected to compete as the European heavyweight representative in the World Open MMA Championship.

"Going to be a long frigging day," he complained to David.

"I'd love to tell you to have a few scoops to help you sleep, son, but I can't recommend it under the circumstances." David responded gleefully as he laced in to his third pint of Guinness in thirty minutes.

"You're a great help. I'm going to call home and check in with the folks."

"You do that. 'I'll be right here but don't be too long, we're boarding shortly. Say 'hi' to them for me."

Finn walked through the terminal searching for an open phone booth. Most of them were occupied by people doing exactly what he intended to do: make a last minute call to some loved one before heading to the US. He knew that most of the people on the plane were heading out there to find work and planned to stay illegally. It was sad. For many of them this would be the last time on Irish soil for a very long time, if not forever.

He dialed his parents' number and chatted with both of them for about fifteen minutes, listening to his mother's admonishments to be careful. He was about to hang up when she said, "Oh that reminds me, Brian Davis called. He wants to speak to you. It sounded important."

She gave him the number and he hung up, promising to call them as soon as he landed in Rio. He tried Brian's number but there was no answer. Someone knocked on the door behind him. David was standing there pointing to his watch mouthing that they had to board now.

He would try again in New York. He walked to the plane with David who by now was extremely happy with life. Finn knew exactly what the drill would be on the plane. David would flirt with the air hostesses and try to get as much alcohol off them as possible. The best Finn could hope for was to get some sleep, or if not that the movie would be good.

He tried to reach David in New York and again In Miami without success. That was extremely unusual. It was after two in the morning in Ireland and he still wasn't answering his phone. Finn resolved to try once more from Rio.

Finn had met Brian quite by accident. He had been competing in a tournament in Dublin almost eight years ago when they were introduced. Brian had turned up to support his English cousin who had come over to participate. Once they started to talk, and realized they both were from Cork, and they hit it off. It didn't take long for them to figure out the other connection between them. Brian's sister was the little girl Finn had helped years ago.

Finn had asked Brian not to mention the fact that they knew each other to Julia immediately. Brian, for his part, thought this was a strange request since Julia would be delighted to meet Finn. Finn couldn't explain why he didn't want Julia to know right away. He wasn't fully sure he knew why. He knew she had boyfriends. Maybe he didn't want to interfere.

Or maybe he was a coward. It was safer to keep his distance than risk rejection.

Someday Brian could tell her—just not yet.

Since there didn't seem to be any harm in it, Brian was happy to comply. Over the years, as their friendship grew stronger, Brian teased Finn about it from time to time about when "someday" would come, but he never broke his word. So Julia had been to her brother, she ended up being oblivious to the fact that one of her brother's best friends was the guy who had saved her years earlier and who remained a hero to her.

Finally, after what seemed like an eternity, they arrived in sunny Rio.

"I cannot wait to go the beach and see all those gorgeous babes in their micro bikinis," David exclaimed with glee not five minutes after the plane touched down. He had lined up a date for himself that night with a very attractive air hostess who he charmed incessantly throughout the flight, but clearly this was not enough for him.

"You are such bum. Do you ever think of

anything else?"

"What else is there to think of, my good friend? Oh, I guess you might have to focus on this tournament thing. Sorry, but for the rest of us, it's the Copacabana all the way."

Finn groaned but his mind was elsewhere. He had convinced himself throughout the flight that Brian was in serious trouble and he was really worried by the fact that he had been unable to get hold of him. Truth be told, he was also concerned that he was now so far away that he was in no position to help out if there really was a problem.

He remembered how amused Brian had been when he had informed Finn that Julia had broken up with her most recent boyfriend and both he and Julia were going to be working in Lissadown. "We're going to be sharing a house. "No way you're getting out of visiting. I'm not skulking around and having clandestine meetings with you behind Julia's back either. You, my friend, will just have to bite the bullet and let her in on the secret. She's going to be majorly pissed off that we kept it from her until now so delaying it any longer will only make things worse when she eventually finds out. And she will find out."

Finn knew he was right. The long awaited "someday" had come. He would have to take the leap risk his heart once and for all. So he'd promised that he would come up for a weekend to stay once he got back Rio. He had used the fact that he was training every weekend as an excuse to postpone the trip but that excuse would be gone soon.

Once they had disembarked, Finn told David

that he was going to make a quick call. He located a phone booth and after two trips to a nearby shop to get the right amount of change and the effort it took to work out all various codes, he finally heard the phone ring. To his great surprise, Brian answered.

"I've been trying to call since yesterday. Is everything okay?"

Brian ignored the question. "Where are you? The line's terrible."

"Sorry. I'm in Rio for the World Open MMA championship. But I'm worried about you. What's up?"

Brian remained quiet for a moment before saying, "Yeah. Everything's fine."

"You're not selling that very well. Tell me what's going on."

"Honestly, it's all good. Focus on the tournament and look me up when you get back. Remember, you promised to come visit." Finn was about to answer when Brian added, "Hey, if something happens to me, promise me you'll look after Julia."

Finn rolled his eyes. As if Brian had to ask that. Finn would look after Julia even if he'd never met Brian. He'd made that vow to himself years ago. But before he could assure Brian that he would, the phone went dead and Finn was left standing there in shock. He knew, despite Brian's protestations, that something was definitely very wrong. He was out of coins and by the time he went back to the shop to get more and dialed the number again, the phone rang out with no response. He could see David hopping around impatiently outside the booth, waiting for him. He put the phone down with a heavy sense of foreboding and went out to join him.

Finn had never said much, if anything, to David about Brian. It just never came up. He had mentioned some time back to Mrs. Kirk during one of his visits to their house about the connection he had made with Brian and how he and Julia were going to be in Lissadown together. There was no point in going into it with David now, and there was nothing he could do for Brian.

~ * ~

Finn progressed through the first three rounds of the tournament without too much difficulty. His fourth fight, in the round of eight, was a different matter. He was pitted against a particularly nasty South African who was well known and disliked for his dirty tactics. Finn's fight with him was a brutal affair and, although he ultimately won a unanimous points victory, the South African had taken him the whole distance and meted out severe punishment along the way.

Finn walked slowly back to the hotel with David after the fight. "I'm not in good shape, man. I've been hit before but this was like nothing I've ever experienced. I need a long bath and a lot of sleep, so no partying for me."

David knew when to be serious and they were at the business stage of the tournament now. "Sounds like a plan, brother. I'll sort out food and I'll make sure you have plenty of bottled water to drink. You've got to stay hydrated."

The next fight was in two days and Finn would need every minute of them to recover. He was still worried about Brian and he had tried again on several occasions to call him, to no avail.

Two days later, when the fight started, Finn was only at eighty percent recovery. He still felt tired and sluggish and there were nagging pains in his lower back and shoulder. He knew this was going to be a tough night, particularly since he was up against an undefeated American named Willie Stone. This guy was a virtual legend in the mixed martial arts world, both for his technique and his toughness. He was renowned for fighting guys from different sports—boxers, wrestlers, judo experts— with great success. He was also the odds-on favorite to win the world title. Finn desperately wished he was in better shape for this fight and he knew if the fight progressed deep into the bout, he was truly screwed. Unlike Litkov, the Russian that Finn had defeated for the European title, Willie Stone was a tremendous natural athlete with great stamina who seemed to get better the longer a fight went on.

The fight started slowly enough with both fighters cagy and showing great respect for the other's ability. When they did engage early on, those encounters were sharp and brutal with each of them absorbing big hits. Almost at the end of the first round, when they were grappling on the floor, Finn felt something go in his shoulder. It had been bothering him since the previous fight but now he was in serious trouble. His opponent didn't seem to notice, which Finn knew was a good thing since otherwise he would just target that shoulder for the remainder of the fight. When he sat in his corner at the end of the round, he said to David, "I'm screwed. My shoulder is fucked up. No way I can get through this."

David just nodded. "What do you want to do? Will we call it quits and stop it now? No one will think badly of you once they know you're injured."

Finn shook his head. "No, I'm going out for the second round. If it gets to a third one, we'll bail. Let's see if I can finish him early in this round."

They both left unsaid that even if Finn won, he wouldn't be able to compete in the final.

"Are you sure? You could do some real damage to yourself."

The bell for the second round sounded. "Just keep an eye out. If it looks really bad out there, tap me out."

"Will do. Good luck. I'm proud of you. We're all proud of you."

For the first minute of the second round, Finn struggled to stay focused. His shoulder was killing him and since he could not use his left arm at all, he was fighting and defending himself with just one hand. This was not a good situation to be in against Willie Stone. Feeling like it was now or never, Finn attacked aggressively and threw his trademark kidney kick twice in rapid succession while delivering a series of blows with his right hand to Stone's face. Sensing there was an opening, he swept Stone onto the mat and quickly sat on him pounding him with his elbow for all his might. Stone tried desperately to unseat him but Finn, mustering up every bit of his strength in his legs, held on tightly.

The blows rained down on Stone's face until it

became a bloodied mess. Once the referee saw that there was no way out for Willie Stone, he stopped the fight and declared Finn the victor. Finn was in such a bad way, he could scarcely understand what was happening and he had to lean on David for support during the victory announcement. He knew for certain that his tournament was over. There would be no final, no crack at becoming world champion.

"I want to go home," was all he said to David in the dressing room afterwards.

David nodded. "I'll make the arrangements but let's get the doctor in to look at you first."

The doctor, who was very experienced and who knew that these guys fought when they were injured, spared Finn a lecture but made sure he knew that wasn't clearing him to fight on.

Finn said nothing. He had made that decision himself anyway.

The good news was that there was no permanent damage done but he would be out for a few months and it would be a very painful rehab. "The price of doing business, doc," Finn had said to him as he shook his hand.

Two days later, they were back in Ireland. Even though Finn had done tremendously well, the trip home had been very subdued. Even David refrained from his usual flirtations. They said very little to each other and slept most of the way.

It was only after Finn had brought his parents up to speed on the tournament and his injury and they were satisfied he was okay, that his mother said, "I'm afraid I have some bad news."

Finn knew what was coming but it was still a shock when he heard that Brian Davis was missing and presumed killed by a notorious criminal gang in Lissadown. There was speculation that Brian had intervened in a gang-related punishment beating and had suffered the consequences for his actions.

Finn was numb. He cursed the fact that he had been in Brazil when he knew Brian was in danger. Intuitively, he knew it wasn't his fault but he felt like he was somehow responsible. His thoughts went to Julia and at that moment, he made his decision. He'd failed Brian, but he'd fulfill his promise. He was going to Lissadown and he was going to make this right.

Chapter Twenty-Eight

Saturday, July 26, 1986
Week Five: Day Six

Finn woke up with a splitting headache. He was devastated. Everything had fallen apart so swiftly. He was furious with Margo but, in his heart, he knew that he was also to blame. He wished he had been upfront with Julia earlier and had told her the whole story, but he had wanted to see if she would fall for him because of who he was and not because of their tangled history.

In reality, he still blamed himself for Brian's death and he had been scared that Julia might too. Rationally, he recognized that this was stupid. There was nothing he could have done, but the concern was still there. Now he had blown it completely.

For the rest of the day, he went through the motions of living. He moved from the farmhouse back into town. He put himself through a hard workout, which he followed up with a long walk.

All in all it was a long, lonely day and he was glad when it was over.

Chapter Twenty-Nine

Sunday, July 27, 1986
Week Five: Day Seven

Sunday wasn't much better. He still felt like a big part of him had been wrenched from his body. Around noon, he put on his running gear and ran out to Roan's facility where he tried to work, largely unsuccessfully, on a report he needed to hand in by Friday. After enduring a couple of frustrating hours, Finn went to the on-site gym where he lifted for an hour then ran home.

A little after six that evening, when he was making some dinner, the doorbell rang. Finn's heart leapt as he hoped and prayed that it might be Julia. He rushed to the door, opened it quickly and saw Mike McGill standing there.

"Uh…Chief Superintendent," he stammered, trying vainly to conceal his disappointment. "What can I do for you?"

McGill looked at him with tired eyes. "You need to come with me to the hospital, Finn. Something bad has happened. Julia's house was petrol bombed last night."

"What? Is she okay? Is she badly burned?"

McGill shook his head. "She's not badly burned. A little bit on her hand and legs. She did inhale a lot of smoke though and they're going to keep her in for a few days observation. She was very lucky. One of my lads out on patrol spotted the smoke and got her out right away. Neighbors came on the scene very quickly and put the flames out, so the house wasn't badly damaged. All in all, she's a very lucky girl."

"Do we know who did this or is that a stupid question?"

McGill nodded. "It was them. Now come on, let's go." He headed down the driveway.

Finn stopped him. "Julia and I had a falling out. Thank you for thinking of me but I doubt very much she'll want to see me."

The Chief Superintendent stopped in his tracks, sighed loudly and without turning around said, "Come on you gobshite. She does want to see you. It was Julia who sent me to fetch you."

Finn was stunned but delighted. He closed the door and raced after McGill.

When they reached the hospital, McGill told him that he placed a cop outside her room and that she would be guarded day and night even though he did not expect there would be any trouble.

Finn thanked him and walked quietly in to the small, private room that Julia had been given. His heart broke when he saw her lying there, eyes covered and both hands heavily bandaged.

"Is that you, Finn?" she asked quietly after a few seconds.

"Yeah, it's me, Julia."

"I thought so." A smile flirted with her lips. "I'd recognize that nice smell of yours anywhere, even here with all the disinfectant. Come over to the bed, please."

Finn approached her and she patted the edge of

the bed for him to sit down. "Listen to me now. I'm so terribly hurt—"

"Julia—"

She waved him quiet. "No. I need to say this. I'm so terribly hurt and I don't know if I will ever be able to trust you again, but I fell in love with you. Being with you was like learning to live again. You brought me back from the deep, dark place I had locked myself in. I thought I'd be there forever, locked away all by myself. But you changed that. You made me laugh, you were kind to me and so very patient. I'll always love you for that.

"But you also hurt me so very much. Those guys who raped me, it was a terrible thing they did to me but they didn't pretend to care for or be nice to me. What you did hurt so much more because I loved you and I expected you to care about my feelings. It's so true what I've said to you before. I'm not a lucky person. For everything good that happens in my life there's a double measure of bad to follow it. I don't know if I can pick myself up again after this one. I don't even know if I want to try. I was thinking earlier, how it might have been better if that cop had not saved me. It might have been the best solution if I hadn't made it out."

"God, Julia, no."

She waved his protest aside. "But I did make it out and there must be a reason for that. What I want now is for you to tell me everything. All of it. The truth, right from the very beginning. In my heart, I can't believe that my brother cried out to you for help and you didn't give it. That does not seem in any way like the Finn I've come to know and love. I need to hear your side of the story. It's the only hope we have of finding a path forward."

Finn sat there stunned, with tears rolling down his cheeks. He was trying to process what she had said. The prospect of her not making it out alive chilled him. But she was right. She had trusted him and he had betrayed her. He'd been too worried about what she'd think of him to tell her the truth about who he was and why he'd come to Lissadown. How was she going to recover from this?

However, he recognized that he had been given a chance to try and make things better, if not right. So he took a deep breath and began to speak. He told her everything, from the very first time they encountered each other all those years ago, to the time in the bar in Cork, to the efforts he had made trying to get hold of Brian when he was on the way to Brazil, all the way up until Friday night, when Margo Kirk had brought their world crashing down around them.

Julia listened, occasionally asking questions but never commenting or passing judgment. He could sense her stiffen when he explained how he was in Brazil when he had spoken to Brian and how her brother had said everything was fine and that they would see each other when he got home. He told her that deep in his heart he knew something was seriously wrong. "You can't be any angrier with me than I am with myself. I'll always regret not catching the next flight home."

"You know that would have been too late anyway if even you had come home then. It wasn't your fault. I want you to know that I don't blame you in any way for what happened to Brian. You hurt me by not telling me the truth, not because you didn't help my brother."

"I'm sorry, Julia. I never meant to hurt you. Far from it. I just thought...I thought. God, I don't know what I thought. I couldn't stand the idea of you hating me for what I'd done. I thought there would be time to tell you everything after..." *I'd made amends.* He couldn't say the words. How could he ever have hoped to *make amends*? He'd been delusional.

"Thank you for telling me. Honestly, I know this was tough but I needed to. I'd like to sleep now."

Then she said the words that gutted him. "Don't come back. I just want to be left alone. You're out of my life. That makes me sad but I can't take any more risks. Please go. I'll have happy memories but that's all it will be between us. Just memories."

Finn stood up. He knew there was nothing more he could say that would make a difference. He was glad that she knew the truth about Brian and that she didn't hold him responsible for his death. It wasn't much but at least he had that to hold onto. He also hoped that with the passage of time there might be an opportunity to win her trust back and he was prepared to put the effort into that.

"Good night, Julia. Thank you for seeing me."

As he walked down the corridor heading for the exit where he knew McGill would be waiting for him, he resolved that he was finally going to finish the job he had come here to do. "This time it's for keeps," he said to himself. "It ends here."

Chapter Thirty

February, 1984
Edgarville, Kentucky

Finn was right. He and Whitney became good friends and although she flirted with him a little on occasion, it was all harmless and more in jest than anything else.

The weeks went by and suddenly he was in his six month. As much as he had enjoyed his time at KenTech, he was ready to go home. He missed his family, his friends and he was eager to return to competitive MMA activity. He had kept up his fitness over the last six months. Indeed, the fitness facilities were so good that he actually believed he was now fitter than he had been at any time in his life.

Two weeks before he was scheduled to depart, Whitney announced that she and Morgan were going to Chicago for a long weekend. They planned to leave on Friday morning and get back on Monday night. This announcement fueled speculation that they were going to get married, as apparently Morgan had been hinting at this to people for the past few weeks. Before she left for the airport, Whitney came over to Finn's lab to say goodbye.

"Have fun, but be safe. Okay?"

She smiled at him and gave him a hug. "Thanks for being such a great friend. I really do love you."

"I know and I love you too."

As she headed to the door of the lab, he called after her.

"Hey Whit, I hope you have a great time."

She stopped and turned to look at him. Then she just shook her head. "I will, yeah."

Finn was a little taken aback by this but he put it down to Whitney just being her quirky Whitney self. He was looking forward to hearing the story of her weekend in Chicago and genuinely hoped that if she was going to marry Morgan that she would be happy. He loved her as a friend and only wanted the best for her. He had had his share of misgivings about her and Morgan but lately things had been going well for the two of them and she seemed very much in love.

On Tuesday morning when neither of them appeared in the lab, speculation intensified. By Thursday morning, when there was still no sign of them nor any word, people were convinced that the happy couple were now in Paris, where Whitney always said she wanted to spend her honeymoon. There were expressions of concern from some quarters who thought it was decidedly out of character for both of them not to contact anyone and share the good news.

Finn was initially a little put out that Whitney hadn't said anything to him but he figured that she was entitled to keep something this big secret. He was looking forward to teasing her when she returned and his biggest concern was that if she was on honeymoon for more than two weeks, he would be back in Ireland before they were back.

"That would be terrible," he admitted to Paul at lunchtime. "I would honestly be devastated if that happened."

Paul, who actually had grown fond of Whitney himself these past few weeks, tried to reassure him. "No way that's going to happen, man. You two are best buds, remember? She wouldn't do that to you. I'm one hundred percent confident that she wants to be the one who organizes your leaving party. There's no way she's going to trust anyone else to do that."

Finn smiled. "I hope you're right."

After a heavy workout, he was back in his apartment shortly before eleven that night when his doorbell rang. He opened the door to see an anxious looking Paul standing there.

"Come in. Is everything okay?"

Paul sat on the couch. Took a couple of deep breaths then looked at Finn with anxiety written all over his face. "I think something really terrible has happened."

Chapter Thirty-One

Saturday, August 9, 1986
Week Seven: Day Six

Julia had been discharged from hospital the next day and returned to work a few days later. Finn had spent the next couple of weeks actively planning his next move. She did not seem to want to speak to him or be anywhere near him. Anytime they encountered each other, she averted her eyes and kept going.

As a result, he stopped going to canteen for lunch. Instead he ate a sandwich alone in his office and caught up on work. He had to smile at the irony. Julia, who for the longest time had been completely ostracized until he came along, was now extremely popular and ate lunch at a packed table every day. He didn't begrudge her this new and improved work environment in any way. He just missed her.

He and his office mate Laura had also done a one-eighty. He was at work, every day, on time and even worked through lunch, while she was often late and had called in sick a couple of times.

"Don't judge," she told him as she rolled in at ten, one Monday morning.

He held up his hands. "I'm in no place to. But are you okay?"

She grinned. "Yeah. I'm having a blast with my new boyfriend. Cam's a great guy, he just doesn't believe in taking life too seriously. I think he's exactly what I needed. I've never really cut loose before." She smiled sheepishly. "It probably comes as no surprise, but I was pretty bookish at university—not a party girl at all. I'm just having a little bit of fun."

"Fun is good. Just be careful that fun doesn't turn around and bite you in the ass."

She rolled her eyes. "Sure, *Mom*. I've got it covered." She snickered. "Or at least, he does."

Finn laughed. "I was thinking more about your job, but that's good too."

It was good to see her having fun. Lissadown had been dark and oppressive for too long. In fact, it was nothing short of remarkable that the petrol bombing of Julia's house hadn't scared people away from her as it would have in the past. This was a sign to him of the progress the whole town had made in the last few weeks.

He was working out very intensely these days and he could feel that his body was nearing peak physical condition. This was crucial because he would only have one shot at getting this right.

Finally, all plans were set. About a month ago, Finn had discovered, quite by accident really, that the four top leaders in the gang met every second Saturday night at a house about five miles outside town. The house was in a pretty remote location with little or no traffic. Although the gang leaders all arrived and left separately, they didn't seem to take any extra precautions.

Finn had driven by the place several times to scope it out and there were no signs of any security measures. *Cocky bastards don't think they need it. This is it. Here's where it will go down.*

Now the day had arrived.

At about seven-thirty that evening, Finn walked into town. He headed to Nutt's Haven, a small bar in the center of town that was usually frequented by Roan employees. When he arrived there, he saw four guys from Roan sitting at a corner table. He walked over, greeted them and offered to buy a round. They agreed enthusiastically. Finn sat with them for about twenty minutes then joined another group, once again buying a round of drinks.

Each time he was at the bar, he took care to speak with as many customers as possible and made sure to tip the barman generously. His plan was simple. He was going to establish his alibi with as many witnesses as possible who could place him in Nutt's Haven and swear that he'd been drinking heavily all night. In reality, he wasn't really touching his drinks at all. He constantly seemed to have a pint that was three quarters empty in his hand with at least another full one waiting there.

As his companions continued to drink more and more pints, it became less and less likely that anyone would notice what he was up to. Over the course of almost three hours, Finn worked the room, constantly making sure that the thirty or so customers in the bar would have clear memories of his presence. He joined in a raucous singsong at one stage and gave a good impression of someone who was beginning to feel the impact of too many pints.

Finally, at ten-forty, he excused himself and headed to the bathroom. He lingered until there was no-one else around then slipped out the side door. It was only used for deliveries and locked from the outside. He would not be able to get back in through that door. He walked steadily down the little lane leading to the river without being noticed.

David Kirk was parked there in a rental car. Finn climbed into the back seat and lay down. Finn had enlisted David's assistance over a week ago without actually filling him in on all the details. David was glad to help and knew enough not to pry too much. He trusted his best friend completely and knew Finn did likewise. That was good enough for him.

"Are we good?" David asked.

"We seem to be. Now let's go. We don't have much time."

Finn changed into an old track suit and sneakers as David drove to the house where the gang members were meeting. "Did you check that everything is still on out there?"

David nodded. "No issues. I was out there less than thirty minutes ago. They look well settled in."

"What about the back window? Were you able to double check it?"

"It's good, Finn. It will open quietly and without effort."

"Great."

David stopped the car down a secluded lane about half a mile from the house and turned off the lights. Finn was going to make the rest of the journey on foot, taking advantage of the darkness and avoiding the risk of the car being spotted.

Before he got out of the car he gripped Dave's

shoulder. "Hey Dave, this wouldn't be able to go down without you."

"Just be careful. Don't take any unnecessary risks. If it's not on, abort and we'll come back another night."

"You got it." Even as he said it, he knew as well as David did that backing out now was not an option unless there were extremely unexpected circumstances.

Finn put two latex gloves on each of his hands and a black skull cap on his head. He nodded at David and quickly got out of the car.

He ran silently in the pitch darkness. He had memorized the route this week and knew exactly where he was going. He ran easily, his body fluid and responsive.

Within minutes he saw the house. There was only one light on in the living room. The rest of the house appeared to be in darkness. *Perfect. Just perfect.* He reached the house, went around to the back and found the window David had opened earlier that day. He listened for a moment but the only sounds were those of muffled voices from the front of the house.

The window opened soundlessly and Finn crawled in carefully. He stopped in the kitchen to make sure nobody had heard him or was moving around the house, then he locked the window. He was going to exit through the front door and he didn't want to leave any sign of a break in.

Here we go. His heart rate increased and the adrenaline began to course through his body. He raced into the front room, surprising the hell out of its occupants and set about his business. He attacked with a rage and a force that surprised even himself but he still managed to stick to his plan and inflict the damage he had set out to cause.

It was all over pretty quickly. As tough as the four gang leaders were, they had never encountered anyone with Finn's combat skills and with the element of surprise completely in his favor, they were no match for him. Once he had completed his task, he walked to the phone and called the emergency services. He gave the address of the house and told the operator there had been an attack and that four people had been severely injured and were in need of ambulances.

He made a point of saying, "It is now eleven thirty-five, how long before the ambulances will get here?"

The operator replied that they were being dispatched now and would be there as quickly as possible.

Finn hung up, even though the operator was still talking. He had established a time for the attack and that was the last thing he needed to do. He took one glance around the room at the four figures all lying crumpled on the floor. They would never create problems for anyone ever again.

Once he had closed the door behind him, he set off running back to the car. This was where all his training and fitness kicked in. He had just expended a huge amount of energy but he still felt loose and alert.

He reached the car, climbed into the back seat and yelled, "Floor it before the ambulance gets here."

David did it without question. In the distance they could hear the approaching sirens but by the time they passed the ambulances, they were on the main road and just one of many cars heading into town.

Finn changed quickly. David had brought damp towels for him to clean himself with and dry ones to finish off. He also had thought of deodorant. *Smart man.*

"All good?" David finally asked.

Finn smiled. "Oh yeah. This will really set the town off once it gets out. Now we just have to get back into town and get me into the pub.

David drove quickly back but not so fast as to attract attention. The last thing they needed was to be stopped for speeding. Once Finn was safely back in the pub, David would drive to West Cork and dump the clothes, shoes and gloves there.

David parked near the pub and they got out. Finn hugged him. "Thanks, brother. I'll never forget this."

David just smiled at him. "Hey, that's what friends are for."

~ * ~

Finn headed up the back alley towards the back door of the pub while David headed towards the front door.

This was the trickiest part. Technically, it was too late for a drink and the pub should be shut. The owners of Nutt's Haven, however, usually took a liberal interpretation of the licensing laws around closing times especially on a Saturday night so there was a hope that David might get in. He knocked quietly on the door and waited.

Nothing.

He knocked again, this time a little louder. Again he waited. *Shit. What do we do now?* He was about to leave when the door opened.

The doorman stood in the doorway. "Sorry mate, we're closed."

"One pint," David pleaded. "My girlfriend just had a baby and I could really murder a pint. Please. Just one."

The doorman stared at him, then cracked a smile. "Boy or girl?"

David grinned. "Boy. A big bruiser at that."

The doorman stood aside. "Congratulations! But just one quick one, okay?"

"Absolutely. Thanks again."

David entered the bar and saw that there were about twenty-five or thirty people there, some of them looking worse for wear. He quickly ordered and paid for a pint then headed to the bathroom. Once he knew the coast was clear, he let Finn in through the side door and left through it himself.

"Travel safely, brother," Finn said and headed into the bar.

~ * ~

Finn reengaged with the various groups he had been with earlier, none of whom seemed to have noticed that he had disappeared for over an hour. He made himself as visible as possible and was among the very last to leave when the pub finally shut down.

"What time is it?" he asked the doorman as he

was leaving, in what he hoped was a voice that sounded drunk.

"Twenty past one in the morning. Time you were in bed."

"I couldn't agree more." Finn laughed and started to walk home pretending to stagger a little while he knew the doorman was watching. "I couldn't agree more."

~ * ~

Earlier that night, Margo Kirk sat in a bar in Cork City. Everything was fucked up with Finn. But what had she done? Nothing, that's what. She'd only told the truth to get the bitch to back off of her man. Since when was telling someone the truth wrong? But the mewling bitch fell apart. *And Finn blames me.* She shook her head. *It's not my fault. I just went after what's mine and now I'm the one out in the cold.*

The guy sitting next her to her had already bought her two drinks and was hitting on her hard. He wasn't much too look at and his breath stank along with the rest of him. She shrugged. *Still, it's better than being alone.*

She leaned closer to him and whispered, "If you come to the ladies bathroom, I'll fuck you there."

He looked at her first in surprise, unsure if she was serious. Then, when she surreptitiously took his hand and slid it up her short skirt, revealing that she wore nothing under it, he looked as if all of his Christmases had come at once.

She winked at him. "I'll go first. You wait outside until I let you know the coast is clear and you come in then."

"You bet." He nodded with a stupid smile plastered on his face, showing his ugly, yellowed teeth.

She shook her head as walked to the bathroom. She'd fuck him but she would not kiss that mouth. Margo hovered in the bathroom impatiently as two women applied makeup and bitched about their husbands. After what seemed like an age they finally left and she motioned to the still-grinning guy who was hanging around outside the door. "Quickly. We can't lock it."

She bent over one of the sinks and lifted her skirt. She felt him enter her and she watched in the mirror as he thrust inside her over and over. Margo looked at her face in the mirror and wondered when it would be over. That was a stupid thing to wonder—it was over very soon.

He grunted, came inside her and immediately pulled out. "Thanks. That was grand."

"Mmm," she mumbled, "it was. You go first. I'll wait a few minutes and meet you back at the bar. I'll take another drink."

"Okay," he said and snuck out.

Margo straightened her skirt, fixed her hair and left just as a woman entered. *Good timing.* When she got back to the bar, he was nowhere to be found. His coat was gone and his drink was empty. "You bastard. Fucking lowlife prick."

She ordered another drink and then another. Eventually, a guy wandered over and started chatting to her. This one bought her three more drinks and she was well on by closing time.

They left the bar together and headed towards Margo's friend's house where she was staying tonight. Margo had made it clear to him that he was going to get lucky tonight. As they passed a laneway, he caught her hand and pulled her into it.

When they were halfway down, he stopped and they started kissing. *At least this one doesn't stink.*

He opened his fly and took out his dick and pushed her head down towards it. "Come on baby, show me what you can do."

Margo took his dick in her hand, stroking it a bit before putting it in her mouth and starting to suck it.

"Oh yeah, baby." He moaned as he started to shove it farther and farther into her mouth with increasing force. By the time he came in her mouth, she was almost choking. When he pulled out, she gagged, spitting out his cum and gasping for air.

"What's the matter, bitch? Isn't it good enough for you to swallow?"

Before she could respond, he swung his fist hard and caught her flush in the jaw. She dropped to the ground and he kicked her twice in the stomach.

"Fucking skanky bitch," he said viciously as he stormed away.

Margo lay there for a few minutes. She could feel the blood flowing from her mouth and she was sure he had broken a rib. She got slowly to her feet. "Fuck you, Finn Lane. This is all your fault. You'll be sorry. Mark my words. You'll be so very sorry."

Chapter Thirty-Two

February, 1984
Edgarville, Kentucky

Paul looked up at Finn and asked if he had anything to drink. The only thing he had was a very expensive bottle of bourbon that he'd planned to bring home to his father as a gift. He poured them both a stiff measure.

Paul chugged almost all of it in one gulp. "Thanks. I needed that."

"Now tell me, why you think something terrible has happened?"

"You know what a radio buff I am."

Finn smiled. "Everyone knows that." Paul liked nothing better than spending hours in the college media studio where there was equipment with which he could tune into radio stations all over the country. He was obsessed with finding remote, obscure stations in the most far-flung parts of the country and listening to local news, sports reports and music. He had obtained special permission from the college to indulge his passion and frequently spent the whole night channel surfing to his heart's content.

"Well, earlier that night, I decided to tune into to some stations in the Chicago area."

"To see if Whitney and Morgan made the news? Why would they?"

"They wouldn't, if everything was okay. I

hoped like hell I wouldn't hear anything."

"But you did?"

Paul nodded. "I found a local news station and listened for a while. They broadcasted a report that a body had been found in a dumpster in a back alley in a dangerous part of the city. The victim was a white female, estimated to be in her mid-twenties. She was about five foot ten with shoulder length blond hair and blue eyes."

"They don't know who she was?"

"No. There was no identification found. She'd been badly beaten and had suffered severe sexual trauma. Her throat had been cut. The police were appealing for witnesses to come forward with any information that might help them identify her or shed some light on the case, how she ended up in the dumpster. They think she was killed four or five days ago."

A chill came over Finn.

"I think it's Whitney," Paul said despondently as Finn refilled their glasses.

Finn wanted to argue against it. The rational side of him knew this description would match hundreds of thousands of American women, but the similarities to how Whitney's mother had been killed were eerie, to say the least. "Look, Paul I'm going to tell you something but you have to keep it to yourself, okay?"

"Absolutely. Do you know something?"

"Not about the case in Chicago, but Whitney told me some things about herself right after I got here. Apparently, her mother—her real mother—was a prostitute in New Orleans and was killed in exactly the same manner."

"You're fucking with me."

"I swear, I'm not."

"Jesus Christ. That's freaky. What the hell. Does it mean something? Could the two of them actually be murdered the same way? What are we going to do?"

"We shouldn't jump to conclusions. Let's go back to the college and see if we can pick up any additional information from that radio station."

After listening to seven different stations over the course of four hours, they finally heard an update. A witness had seen a woman matching that description on Sunday night in a bar not far from the dumpster where the body had been found. She had been in the company of an unidentified white male who looked like he was also in his mid-twenties. He was about six feet tall, well built, with dark brown or black hair.

Paul looked at Finn in horror. "That sounds like Morgan."

Finn stood up and paced the room. He wanted to disagree; just like the description of the victim, it could be anyone. But he couldn't. Something deep within him knew the victim was Whitney and if it was, the man was Morgan.

"Fuck, fuck, fuck," was all he could say. Still, he didn't want to believe it.

They stayed there until the morning listening for more news on the case. Hoping, praying that the victim would be identified as some other poor girl. But there were no further updates.

Paul switched the equipment off. "We have to

go to the cops. It might not be her, but we won't know unless we tell them."

Finn nodded. "But let's go over to the labs first and see if they've turned up or if there's been any word from them. Maybe we've been worried all night for nothing. If no one has heard anything, we'll go to the cops."

They only news they learned at the lab was bad news. There had been no word from Whitney or Morgan. But Morgan's parents had called several times looking for him. It had been over a week since they last heard from him and they had become worried, since they were expecting him to call on Monday. Finn knew no one would be calling about Whitney. She was estranged from her parents.

Finn turned to Paul. "I want to tell Spaulding first. He has a right to know."

The professor was shocked and upset. "You're right though, you need to report this to the police, even if it is just to assure ourselves it isn't Whitney. But, Finn, keep this to yourself. This could all still be a tragic coincidence. You don't want to ring alarm bells only for the two of them to turn up safe and sound after partying for the week."

Finn and Paul went to the local station and told them every detail they knew. The detective said he'd relay the information to the Chicago police department and would get back in touch if he needed anything else.

Finn had planned to go and take a nap but when he got to the apartment, he knew he wouldn't be able to sleep so he changed and went for a long run which he followed up with a grueling session in the gym. He could see people looking at him strangely as he worked out with such ferocity, but no one approached him or said anything.

The next few days ground by interminably. The tension and concern in the department was palpable as rumors started to leak that something bad might have happened Whitney.

On Monday afternoon, Finn was in the lab trying to wrap up the last of his work when he looked up from his desk to see a visibly shaking Paul standing there in the company of two grim-looking police officers. His heart sank like a stone and a lump rose in his throat.

"Is there somewhere private we can speak?" one of officers asked.

Finn nodded. He stood up shakily and walked in a daze to the little break room that the post grad students used. There were four students already there but they left silently when Finn asked if they could have the room.

"I'm afraid we have some very bad news. We relayed the information you provided to our colleagues in Chicago. They were able to access Whitney's dental records through her foster parents. A positive identification had been made. The body found in the dumpster was indeed Whitney Campbell."

Although Finn had been expecting the worst, actually hearing the officers confirm that Whitney had been murdered shook Finn to the core. He sat there, too stunned to say anything. Filling his thoughts was that wonderful night in Lexington when he had held Whitney in his arms, as they listened to Bruce sing *Thunder Road.* He remembered the warmth of her body against his as they swayed slowly to the music and how her eyes had shone with tears when the song ended. She had been truly happy at that moment. And now she was gone. Brutally murdered and dumped in a back alley, just like her mother.

He barely heard the officer say that they were still searching for Morgan Herman, who seemed to have vanished without a trace; that Whitney's foster parents were on their way to Chicago to formally identify the body and bring her back to New Orleans to be buried; that Morgan Herman's parents were also flying to Chicago to aid the search for their son who was now the prime suspect in Whitney's murder.

The officers offered their condolences, shook their hands and left. Paul and Finn just sat there. Eventually, Finn got to his feet and said, "I'm going to tell Spaulding. He'll need to let the others know."

Chapter Thirty-Three

Sunday, August 10, 1986
Week Seven: Day Seven

The Sunday morning news report stunned the people of Lissadown. As more and more radios were turned on, the breaking headlines completely upended normal routines. The early morning report first revealed that the four alleged leaders of a ruthless criminal gang based in Lissadown had been attacked and severely assaulted. All four were reported to be in hospital in critical but stable condition.

By mid-morning, the report was updated and details of the extent of their injuries were provided. The four men were now thought to have suffered near identical injuries: their spines had been broken, their hands crushed, their eyes gouged out and most remarkably, their tongues had apparently been ripped from their mouths. While it was thought that all four men would survive, it was clear according to the news reporter that they would be totally incapacitated for the rest of their lives.

At noon, a further update added that it was now clear that it appeared a single assailant had been involved in the assault and that no weapons were used.

Like virtually everyone else in Lissadown, Julia sat there glued to her radio, eagerly awaiting each update. As the news continued to unfold and the picture of what had actually happened became clearer, she became more contemplative.

After the noon report, she switched the radio off and sat for a long time thinking. Then, having reached a decision, she stood up, went upstairs and packed a small travel bag with clothes and toiletries. Just before three, Julia locked her house behind her and headed to her car. On second thought, she decided it was better to leave the car at her house, so she slung the bag over her shoulder and started walking.

It was a bright, crisp afternoon with blue skies and wispy clouds. There were people everywhere, most huddled together in groups, holding intense conversations. What struck Julia most forcibly was the amount of laughter she heard coming from these groups as she passed by. There was an overwhelming sense of joy and relief in the air and everyone seemed to be in an exceptionally good mood. Along the way, she smiled and greeted people she knew and even some she didn't, as she was subjected to multiple versions of, "Great day, isn't it?"

As she approached her destination, she grew more and more anxious. This could be a huge mistake. She had no clue how she would be received and she certainly wasn't confident she had the courage to see her plan through.

She stood at the door for what seemed like an age, took a deep breath then rang the bell.

When Finn opened the door, his expression told Julia she was probably the last person he had expected to see standing there. He looked at her, stunned into silence.

She smiled at him. "You're doing that fish out of water thing again. I told you before, it's not at all attractive. Can I come in?"

Finn clamped his mouth shut and stood aside to let her pass. They went into kitchen. "Tea? Coffee? Water? Something stronger?" he asked.

"I would love a gin and tonic right now, but I'll stick with tea. Thanks."

They both were silent while Finn made tea and it was only when they were seated at the table that Julia began to speak. "I was wrong. I was so very wrong. You are the very best thing that has ever happened to me in my miserable life and all I did was push you away. Yes, you hurt me by not telling the truth from the start, but that isn't an excuse. I should have listened to your explanation and most importantly, I should have trusted you. You had never given me a reason not to trust you. You had your reasons for not telling me. You believed they were valid and I don't think you intended to hurt me. After your patience and kindness with me, I didn't give you a chance, and that's where I messed up. I'm so sorry and I hope you can forgive me."

"Dear God, Julia, there is nothing to forgive. I messed up too."

She smiled weakly. "Now, I don't know—and I don't need to know—if that was you last night. Whether you did or didn't, all I know is that you made the first steps. If it wasn't you, you were the catalyst for whoever it was. You have given this town back to the people, you've given everyone a chance at a normal life and families the opportunity to be together again." She captured his gaze. Her eyes were filled with tears. "I love you for that too."

She took a deep breath and stood up. "Can I use your bathroom?"

Finn just nodded, seemingly unable to find a response to her words. Fish out of water again. That was her Finn.

Julia's heart was pounding when she leaned against the wall of the bathroom. As difficult as it had been to say those words, she knew that the biggest and riskiest challenge was about to come. She splashed cold water on her face and stared at her reflection in the mirror. This was the thing she had feared most from the start and she had to get it over with. She wouldn't risk her heart again, without knowing.

She walked back into the kitchen, firmly resolved to see this through.

Finn stood there in the middle of the room. "Julia, are you okay? Is something wrong?"

"I'm fine. But I need you to turn away and don't turn back around until I ask you to, Okay?"

"Okay."

She quickly undressed, removing every stitch right down to her socks and shoes and placing them on the counter behind her. She stood there completely naked, about to make the single biggest decision of her life. This was it. All at once. Ripping the bandage off. Jumping into the water head first. In a moment she would know.

"Now you can turn around now."

~ * ~

Finn had no idea what was happening but he'd

learned letting her navigate was usually best. When she asked him to turn around, he wasn't sure what to expect.

There she stood, completely bared to him. And finally, he understood the magnitude of what this meant. He looked at her body, at each of the scars and burns that disfigured her breasts, her abdomen and legs.

"You need to see it all," she said softly and began to turn slowly so he could see the extent of the damage to her back, buttocks and legs. When she had turned back to him again he saw the look of determination in her eyes. Her body had been her biggest insecurity. He knew she had summoned every ounce of courage to do this, to simply stand in front of him.

Finn walked over to her and wrapped her in his arms. "You are beautiful. I've never seen anything as beautiful in my life. And so very strong, and brave. There are no words."

Julia held onto him tightly and whispered, "Take me upstairs and make love to me."

"You're certain?"

She nodded. "I'm giving this gift. It isn't being taken from me."

Finn reached out and swept her easily into his arms. He looked into her eyes and he could see the trust in them. Without a word, he carried her out of the kitchen and upstairs to his bedroom where he placed her gently on the bed.

He undressed slowly in front of her then laid next to her on the bed.

She caressed his cheek and looked into his

eyes. "Be patient, please. This is my first time of my own free will."

"Oh my beautiful girl, you don't need to ask." He leaned down and kissed her lips. Then his kisses strayed down the slender column of her neck, to her breasts. Julia flinched when his lips met the first scar.

"Shh," he whispered. "Let me show you the beauty and strength I see."

He waited, unwilling to move another inch without her permission.

She nodded he lowered his head again, and gently kissed every scar as he traveled down her body.

When he reached her mound, he caressed it lightly. "Will you open for me, Julia?"

She parted her legs. Taking it as assent, he spread them wider, again kissing the scars on her belly and inner thighs.

He kissed her mound before sliding his tongue in, tasting her salty wetness and barely touching the sensitive nub there.

She gasped, then sighed and relaxed.

"That's my girl. Let me take you to ecstasy."

He continued to give her pleasure, alternately licking and sucking her clit until she was panting and moaning. He slid one finger inside her and then two, watching for any sign that it caused her distress.

To his delight, she seemed to have lost herself in her rising pleasure.

He held her on the edge until she arched against him.

"Please, Finn, I don't think I can stand this anymore."

That was all the invitation he needed. He positioned himself between her knees and entered her slowly, all the time looking into her eyes. Although it might kill him to do so, if he saw one hint of fear or pain he would stop.

His needn't have worried. She writhed under him, taking as much pleasure as she gave and crying out with abandon when she climaxed. Only then did he find his own release.

They lay in each other's arms quietly for what seemed like ages.

No words were necessary.

Finally Julia broke the silence. "I was so afraid you'd be turned off by me. I never thought I'd have the courage to be naked in front of anyone again, never mind making love."

Finn stroked her hair gently for a moment before kissing the top of her head. "I love you, Julia Davis. I have since I was a boy and I always will. You are the most beautiful woman in the world to me, inside and out."

She kissed him, rose up on her elbow and grinned. "Well if you really love me, take me out for a drink and a bite to eat. I'm starving and I can already taste a gin and tonic."

He laughed. "You got it. Let's take a walk to The Shack."

Ten minutes later, Finn held Julia's hand as they headed to the pub. He couldn't find words to describe the sense of elation he felt. He leaned over and kissed her happily.

"Oooh kissy, kissy," a voice yelled out from behind them.

They spun around and saw three boys of about twelve sitting on a wall.

"Go on, give her another one," said one with red hair and a freckled faced. "I know you want to."

"I believe I will, because you are so right." He kissed her again and they walked on with the cheers of the boys trailing behind them.

Once they reached The Shack, the pub was busy though not full—it was still early. Julia said, "I'll get a table. Make mine a double and get some sandwiches and crisps and nuts. In fact, get anything you can. I'm starving."

Finn went to the bar and placed the order as he pulled out his wallet.

The barman, Mark, looked him squarely in the eye, frowning. "You know I can't let you pay for anything, right? Even if I didn't put it on the house, there isn't a single person here who would let you pay."

Finn thought about arguing but decided against it, simply replying, "Thanks, Mark."

He turned around, leaned against the bar and looked for Julia. He could see her sitting at a table talking to an old lady who held her by the hand. The old lady's face was full of emotion but he could that she was smiling.

When he arrived at the table with their drinks and enough food for six people, the old lady was gone. "What was that all about?" he asked.

Julia practically inhaled a sandwich before replying. "Jesus, I needed that. I haven't eaten in two days. That was Mary Browne. She lost two sons in the past two years to gang violence and her youngest had to move to London. She spoke to him earlier and he's planning to come home now that the coast is clear. There's going to be a lot of that happening in Lissadown now." She took his face in her hands. "All thanks to you."

Finn didn't answer her. There was no point. He wasn't going to lie to her or pretend that he didn't do it. Not this time.

After a couple of very pleasant hours in The Shack, much of which was spent attempting to dissuade happy customers from buying them even more drinks, Finn and Julia left the pub. "Will I walk you home or back to my house?"

"Back to your house. And before you ask, yes, I am planning on spending the night. I brought some things with me."

"I wondered what was in the bag."

"Well now you know. You can drive me to work too. Won't that be nice?"

Finn laughed. "You were very confident of the outcome of your little venture, weren't you, dearest."

Julia stopped and looked up at him, very seriously. "Actually, no I wasn't. I was scared silly and I honestly had no idea how you'd react after I'd been so horrible to you. And I sure didn't know what you'd think when you saw me naked. Do you know, I have no mirrors in my house other than the small one in the bathroom? I never look at my body anymore. I can't bear to see what they did to me."

Finn squeezed her hand. "I meant what I said.

Completely. You are beautiful and I want to see you naked all the time. In fact, let's walk faster. It's already been too long since the last time."

She laughed. "Now look who's confident of a positive result."

But she picked up the pace.

~ * ~

It hadn't been a quiet Sunday for Mike McGill. Early that evening he received a report of a demonstration outside the home of another senior gang member. Mike deployed the riot squad and arrived to find a crowd of about forty townspeople surrounding the house and chanting, "Out. Out. Out. Out."

Before his men could take any action, the gang leader came rushing out of the house, brandishing an axe. "Fuck off the lot of you," he screamed. "Do you know who you're fucking with? I'll make you very sorry."

Brendan Macken walked to the head of the crowd and stood there in front of the gang leader. "We're not afraid of you anymore. Just pack up and leave."

The gang leader raised the axe over his shoulder as if preparing to take a swing at Brendan. The riot squad moved in. Brendan Macken was pushed to the ground in the melee. An officer stood over him with a baton and shield.

Mike felt a twinge of shame in his gut when Macken put his hands on his head as if fearing the officer was there to support the gang member.

When the axe-wielding gang member had been restrained, the officer turned his attention to

Brendan. "Sir, are you all right? Let me give you a hand up."

Brendan appeared surprised, but took the man's hand. "I was sure you were going to hit me."

The riot squad officer stared at Macken for a moment. "Why would I hit you, sir? I'm here to protect you." He reached out his hand and shook Macken's. "Have a nice day, sir."

None of the protesters had been injured, but the gang leader had not fared as well and was sitting handcuffed in the squad car with a bloodied head.

Mike McGill watched the whole exchange and smiled to himself. The healing had begun.

~ * ~

When they reached Finn's house he flipped on the television and sat on the couch.

Julia looked at him askance. "You want to watch TV?"

He smiled and pulled her onto his lap. "Just for a minute. I want to see the news."

Not surprisingly, the lead story was about the attack. It seemed to have captured the whole country's attention.

"It has been confirmed that one of the four men brutally assaulted in a private residence outside of Lissadown is the alleged kingpin of a particularly violent criminal gang operating in the area, and the other three are his lieutenants. All four are stable but still in critical condition. A spokesperson from the Regional Hospital would not speculate as to their prognosis, but sources close to the case have described the injuries as 'devastating', suggesting that it is unlikely that any of them will ever speak or walk again, or regain any vision. Even the use of their hands will likely be limited due to the severe damage done. Normally, in cases like these it is common to see a widespread outpouring of sympathy. However, more allegations of atrocities committed by the gang are coming to light by the hour.

"Earlier this evening Joe Delany, Associate Director of Public Prosecutions for this region, spoke with reporters outside his home."

The coverage cut to video of the interview.

A reporter asked, "Mr. Delany, in light of the recent allegations of atrocities committed by or at the behest of the four victims, do you believe a crime has been committed?"

Delany almost sneered back at the reporter. "How can you ask such an inane question? Of course a crime has been committed. Four men were brutally beaten to within an inch of their lives and will spend the rest of their days in darkness, unable to speak or walk. This was a crime and the perpetrator will be brought to justice."

Another reporter asked, "Do you have any suspects or any idea how this attack could have been perpetrated?"

"All of the damage appeared to be inflicted without the use of weapons. The person responsible would have to be extremely strong and an absolute expert in martial arts. Frankly, I doubt there's more than one or two people in the country capable of doing this."

Julia frowned. "He might as well have broadcasted your name. He couldn't have identified you any clearer than that."

"Yes, and he looks like he's loaded for bear."

"Are you worried? Because I am. I've seen how the police do the dirty work for these guys."

"I am a little." He shrugged. "But there's not much we can do about it now."

They turned their attention back to the news report.

"Mr. Delany, do you have any other comments regarding this case?"

The prosecutor looked directly into the camera. "Yes, I do. I want to make it perfectly clear to this audience and the people of this country: If you have any sympathy for the perpetrator of this heinous act, then you are on the wrong side of the law. This was a crime, make no mistake about it, and we will prosecute whoever did this to the fullest extent possible. Anyone caught aiding and abetting this criminal will also be prosecuted and receive the maximum sentence allowable by law. Mark my words. Finally, let me tell you that we are pursuing a definite line of enquiry and expect to make an arrest very shortly."

~ * ~

Chief Superintendent McGill switched off the television and looked at his wife. "What a load of bullshit. He'll get no support from the police on this. Yes, we'll do our jobs, but no one is going to pursue this vigorously."

"What definite line of enquiry is he talking about?"

Mike shook his head. "There is none. There was no evidence whatsoever. There weren't even any signs of a break-in. It could have been an inside job for all we know since they appeared to have let the attacker in. We have nothing concrete that links anyone to the scene."

That was true. However, Mike knew exactly what Delany was doing. He was building a circumstantial case against Finn Lane.

Chapter Thirty-Four

February, 1984
Three Years Earlier

Less than hour after Finn had broken the sad news of Whitney's murder in Chicago to Professor Spaulding, he assembled all of the chemistry post grad students in one of the labs.

"I suspect by now most of you have heard the news about Whitney Campbell. She was indeed found murdered in Chicago."

No one spoke for a moment. In fact, the only sounds were sobs that escaped from Whitney's heartbroken friends.

Professor Spaulding continued. "Whitney was unique in so many ways. She was a smart, generous, beautiful, young woman. Outgoing and personable, she never met a stranger. While she came to KenTech on an athletic scholarship, it became immediately obvious that she was, in fact, a scholar. Her work here as a postgrad has contributed in a very meaningful way to our research. Her sparkling personality, skills and zest for life will be sorely missed."

He paused for a moment, appearing to consider his next words. "I am certain that you are also aware that Morgan Herman is missing and considered a suspect in Whitney's murder. Please remember that he is only a suspect. There is still very little information and it is possible that Morgan too is a victim."

This last part was a hard sell to the majority of the assembled students who had by now decided that Morgan was completely guilty. Finn was still unsure. He had to admit that this seemed like the most realistic scenario but he found it hard to come up with a motive.

Was it possible, in the heat of some argument, that Morgan had committed a crime of passion? Did he stage Whitney's body to look like her mother's in an attempt to draw suspicion away?

If not that, the alternative was nearly unthinkable. Morgan undoubtedly knew the circumstances of Whitney's mother's murder. Could he have been so cold-blooded to have planned it in advance?

Finn didn't want to go there. Just as Spaulding said, it was possible that it was all just a tragic coincidence and that Morgan's dead body could still turn up somewhere else. Finn's head hurt. He didn't know what to think.

Professor Spaulding finished by telling everyone that there would be a memorial service that evening at the college for Whitney and that the funeral was to be held the following Tuesday in New Orleans. Finn was supposed to be back in Ireland by then but he changed his plans. Whitney had been important to him and he was going to attend the funeral.

The memorial that evening ran the full gamut of emotions. There were moments of intense sadness, laughter and even happiness as friends and teachers remembered Whitney. A number of musicians turned up, playing a variety of music—some soft and reflective, others bright. In a way, Finn felt the mixture resembled Whitney herself.

The turnout was immense as virtually every student at KenTech knew or knew of Whitney Campbell. A number of former classmates turned up as well as did members of the all- conquering tennis team. Whatever disagreements or disapprovals that people had were put aside for the night.

Finn wore one of the Bruce Springsteen tee-shirts he had bought at the concert. He remembered how Whitney had teased him that he had to think of her every time he wore one. He doubted that the circumstance under which he was doing so tonight had entered her mind when she had said it.

~ * ~

Finn and Paul traveled together to New Orleans. The hardest part for Finn was the viewing. The undertaker had done an outstanding job. Whitney looked as beautiful as possible under the circumstances. There were no signs of bruises or the mark on her throat. Finn just stood there and looked at her with a heavy heart. It had only been six months but he had gotten to know her so well.

Paul had been right, Whitney had become Finn's *best bud* at KenTech and he loved her very much. After a moment, he reached out and touched her. "I'll see you, Whitney," was all he said before walking quickly out of the room.

Whitney was buried the next day. Morgan Herman's parents turned up but were mostly shunned by people who considered their son guilty of Whitney's murder.

Finn made a point of going to speak to them and sympathizing with them. They were also heartbroken, for they had lost a child as well. They just didn't yet know the circumstances, if they ever would. Finn pitied them. If their son turned up alive, he was most likely a killer and could face the death penalty. If their son turned up dead, he was as much a victim as Whitney. Either way, the road ahead was a hard one.

Whitney's foster parents, though they had suffered a tragic loss, at least had closure. Finn had never learned why she had estranged herself from them. He had asked on several occasions but each time she shut down the conversation swiftly. They seemed like very nice people. It must be killing them that they had only reconnected with her through her death.

Three days later, Finn said his goodbyes to everyone and packed up to head home. There had been no send-off party at his request. He couldn't contemplate the idea of one without Whitney being there. Paul drove him to the airport. They didn't speak much on the way. Finn couldn't help thinking about the contrast between this journey and the one he had made with Whitney on his first day.

At the airport, he embraced Paul, thanked him for being such a good friend and boarded his flight.

Chapter Thirty-Five

Monday, August 11, 1986
Week Eight: Day One

Finn woke up at the crack of dawn as usual. He thought briefly about getting up and doing his normal routine, starting with a workout. But then he looked at Julia lying fast asleep next to him and decided against it. He wasn't ready to leave this haven. He snuggled closer to her.

She groaned. "Is it time to get up? Please say no."

"It's not. Go back to sleep."

Later as they drove out to Roan, Julia was oddly quiet.

"Something on your mind?"

"I'm just wondering what people are going to say this morning."

"About what?"

"About you. About me. About us. I suspect there will be a lot of questions."

"It's all good. I'll just say I saw you walking out and stopped to give you a ride."

"Yeah, that'll work, genius." She chuckled. "Good luck with that."

Julia was right. They did cause quite a stir. When people had left work on Friday, it was clear that Finn and Julia were not even on speaking terms and now on Monday they were driving to work together like the happiest couple in the world. This coupled with the universally held view that Finn was responsible for the attacks on Saturday night, made for plenty of gossip.

Laura, who as usual for a Monday looked a bit worse for wear, could hardly contain herself. "Sooooo, how was your weekend?"

"Quiet. I had too many pints on Saturday night in Nutt's Haven so I basically laid low yesterday. How was yours? You and the boyfriend still at it? By the way, when am I going to get to meet him?"

She ignored his question. "So, if your weekend was so quiet, how did you end up driving Miss Julia to work?"

"Her car broke down," he deadpanned.

"Liar. But I'm too tired to argue so I'll give you a pass this time."

The rest of the day passed by in a blur. Finn decided not to risk going to the canteen so he ate in his office. On his way to make a cup of coffee, he bumped into Brendan Macken.

"Finn, there you are. I thought you might be interested to know, six machine operators didn't show up for work today."

Finn adopted a neutral expression. "Really?"

"And if you ask me, they'll never be back." A big grin spread across his face. "Things just get better and better."

Finn nodded, but didn't respond.

Brendan didn't seem to need a response as he kept right on talking. "By the way, it was good to see you in Nutt's Haven on Saturday night. You looked like you were having a grand old time sculling pints to beat the band. I was actually still there myself when you left. I remember thinking it's a good night on the town that doesn't end until after one in the morning." Brendan smiled and nodded his head thoughtfully. "One o'clock, right enough. I guess it wasn't you after all who did the deed on those four. There's no one capable of being in two places at one time. And there was a bunch of us who saw you there. We remember that very clearly. Very clearly, indeed. You were there all night, sure." He looked at Finn for a moment then put out his hand.

Finn took it and they shook.

"You're a good man, Finn. We all know that."

Finn met Julia by the front entrance a little after five that evening and they walked to his car together.

Once safely ensconced in the car, Julia glanced sideways at him. "Interesting day. Very interesting."

He gave her a mischievous grin. "Well I hope the night is even more interesting."

"One track mind." She frowned but her eyes twinkled.

"Shall we pick up take-away or just get straight to the interesting evening?"

She laughed. "How about you drop me at my house first? I'll cook something for dinner and afterwards we can head back to your place. I need clothes for tomorrow and clean knickers."

Finn opened his mouth but she put up a hand. "Don't you say it. I know exactly where your filthy mind is going."

"Okay. Clean knickers." He winked at her. "So

as long as I get to pick them out."

She laughed again. It was a sound he hadn't heard enough of and was beginning to crave.

He drove to Julia's house and leaned over to give her a kiss before she got out of the car. "Mmmm. That tastes like more."

"Consider it a starter. Be back by seven-thirty."

He sighed. "Okay. Seven-thirty."

She got out of the car but leaned her head back in and gave him another quick kiss. "Don't be late. And I promise, later, I'll make it worth your while."

"Ah, punctuality may become my newest virtue."

She laughed and waved before entering her house.

This was perfect. It would give him plenty of time to get changed and pick up a nice bottle of wine.

At six forty-five, Finn's doorbell began ringing incessantly, as if someone were leaning on it.

"Someone's eager," he muttered as he headed to the door. He opened it to find Mike McGill and six other police officers standing there.

McGill looked grim. "Finn Lane, I'm arresting you on suspicion of assault with the intention of causing grievous bodily harm. You are not obliged to say anything unless you wish to do so, but whatever you say will be taken down in writing and may be given in evidence. Please turn around, so that my officers can handcuff you."

McGill was clearly upset, as if this was the last thing he wanted to do.

Finn wouldn't make it harder. He turned

around and joined his hands together. McGill gave instructions for him to be handcuffed but none of the police officers moved. Finn guessed they weren't too keen on it either.

"Do it now," McGill snapped.

An officer stepped forward and muttered, "Sorry, Finn," before handcuffing him.

As they escorted him to the awaiting vehicle, Finn turned to McGill. "Can you do me a favor, please, Chief Superintendent? Julia is waiting for me at her house. She's cooking dinner and expecting me in about thirty minutes. Can you tell her what has happened, please? I don't want her to get worried when I don't show up."

~ * ~

Finn's request tore at McGill's heart. "Sure, Finn." He instructed his officers to escort Finn to the station for processing before climbing into his own car. As he drove to Julia's house, he reflected on the day's events that had led to Finn's arrest.

Midmorning, word had come down that Finn was to be arrested on suspicion of assault. He'd asked what evidence was being used to support the arrest, but was quickly shut down. Not put off, he'd called the Police Commissioner, making a case for not arresting Finn too hastily. He argued that there was no evidence and that emotions were running very high in the town. He feared, in the absence of solid evidence, an arrest would trigger public unrest. The Commissioner agreed with McGill but he maintained that orders were orders and had to be followed.

When McGill walked to Julia's door, he was

certain he'd be faced with angry tears, but to his surprise, she was quite sanguine about Finn's arrest and genuinely didn't seem angry or upset with him.

"You do know there are witnesses who will swear that he was in Nutt's Corner all night until after one in the morning. Unless, you can place him at the scene, I don't know how you can hold him."

"We'll look into everything, Julia. I promise."

~ * ~

Julia was heartbroken that Finn had been arrested, but she did not despair. She was confident that, lacking any evidence against him, he would be released. She turned on the television to watch the news, hoping to hear more about whatever case they felt they had against him.

The broadcast led with the shocking story of Finn's arrest. This time Joe Delany was in the studio for the interview, looking smug and self-satisfied. "This is a big night for justice." He practically crowed. "It just goes to show how efficient this office is at prosecuting criminals."

The reporter didn't appear convinced. "That's interesting to hear you say that, when your office has been accused of *not* following up on criminal activity in Lissadown in recent years and of even turning a blind eye to criminal activity by the very gang these men are alleged to be members of. How do you respond to that?"

"Absolute nonsense," a clearly annoyed Delany blustered. "I won't dignify that comment with a response."

The news show then went live to Declan Byrne, the Midlands reporter in Lissadown.

"Declan, I believe you've discovered some information pertinent to this case?"

"Yes that's right. Two witnesses have come forward who can vouch for Dr. Lane's whereabouts on the night in question. I'm here with Brendan Macken and Niall Murphy, both of whom were in a pub with Dr. Lane on Saturday night when the attack took place. Mr. Macken, can you tell us what you know?"

Brendan Macken looked steadily into the camera and began to speak in a calm and measured voice. "Finn Lane is innocent of this charge. He was in Nutt's Haven on Saturday night from before eight until after one in the morning. I saw him, Niall saw him too and so did many others. As soon as we're done here, I'm heading over to the police station to sign an affidavit, swearing that I was with Finn in Nutt's Haven at the time of the attack. Niall here is going to as well and I'm calling now for everyone else who was there on Saturday night to do the same. This man needs our assistance. We must stand up and be counted now. For too long, we've been afraid and stayed silent. No more. No longer. Join me and Niall. If you were in Nutt's Haven on Saturday night, go to the police station and sign the affidavit. Do it tonight. Put an end to injustice in this town."

Declan Byrne turned back to the camera. "Well, powerful stuff indeed. Back to you in the studio."

The reporter addressed Delany. "Mr. Delany, how do you respond to the fact that there are at least two witnesses, and maybe more, willing to swear an oath that Finn Lane could not have carried out the attack?"

"Quite simple," Delany snapped angrily. "They're lying."

The reporter's eyebrows shot up. *"They're lying?"* His voice was incredulous. "Why would they do that? Our sources maintain you have no physical evidence against Dr. Lane placing him at the scene. And yet, you discount statements from credible witnesses who can place him elsewhere. How can you defend that?"

Delany stared at him coldly. "I'm not going to comment on what evidence we have or make any further statements."

The reporter turned to the cameras. "Clearly, there's a lot more to this unfolding story so stay tuned, we'll update you as we learn more."

Chapter Thirty-Six

Tuesday, August 12, 1986
Week Eight: Day Two

If Brendan Macken thought for one moment that his televised plea would result in the thirty or so patrons of Nutt's Haven last Saturday night going to the station to sign an affidavit in support of Finn Lane, he had sorely miscalculated.

Of course, he hadn't counted on Lissadown's small, weekly newspaper, *The Lissadown Examiner*. The paper was published locally every Tuesday and was largely ignored by the majority of people in the town. That changed when it printed an editorial commentary right on the front page:

> *It has been suggested that there were approximately thirty people in Nutt's Haven last Saturday night who can vouch for Finn Lane's presence during the time the attack for which he has been accused took place. It was further proposed that those approximately thirty people were honor bound to sign a sworn affidavit testifying to this.*
>
> *This newspaper disagrees.*
>
> *Rather, it is the view of this newspaper that there were not approximately thirty people in that bar on Saturday night.*

Instead, we believe that every decent citizen of this country was present in Nutt's Haven on Saturday night. Therefore, this newspaper believes that it's the duty of every decent citizen of this country to sign that sworn affidavit testifying to their presence there.

To do otherwise is tantamount to accepting that injustice should be allowed to continue unchecked and unfettered.

To do otherwise continues to give free rein to evil men to perpetrate their evil deeds on ordinary, decent citizens.

To do otherwise sends a message that we are unwilling and afraid to stand up for justice and the right to lead a normal life.

To do otherwise is to disrespect all of the men, women and children who have suffered at the hands of evil thugs.

To do otherwise is to abandon the hope that was beginning to shine in our town.

This newspaper believes now is the time to rise up and let our voices be heard. Now is the time to look evil in the face and say, "No More."

The staff of this newspaper wishes to make it known that we were all present in Nutt's Haven on Saturday night and we are witnesses."

About an hour after the paper was published, a woman from Lissadown called into the top-ranked radio show in the country and read the editorial over the air where it was heard by over half the country. Within minutes, signs started to appear in the windows of shops, offices, factories, hotels, schools, hospitals and homes all carrying the same message: "We were in Nutt's Haven on Saturday night and we are witnesses."

Within an hour, residents of Lissadown were lining up to sign affidavits. By ten the next morning, there were almost a hundred people in line waiting to sign. By noon, the number had grown to over five hundred and stretched out from the police station past the Cathedral, along the wall of the army barracks and out beyond the old Lissadown railway station. By then, the number of signatories who swore they were in Nutt's Haven, with Finn Lane at the time of the attack on Saturday, was over four hundred.

And still they came.

First it had been townspeople, then as news trickled out, people from surrounding areas joined the queue. Once the story had been picked up by the media, people started to come from all over the country.

In the middle of the afternoon, every single employee of Roan Pharmaceuticals marched from the plant to the center of Lissadown to sign their names. As they passed, workers from other companies in the industrial estate joined them. Shops and pubs along the route were shut as more and more people joined in.

Pupils from the local secondary school began to walk out of their classes, ignoring their teachers' threats and orders to get back to their desks until finally the teachers joined the march too.

Declan Byrne and his camera crew filmed the growing phenomenon and the pictures were beamed to television sets around the country, spurring even more people to head to Lissadown. By six, over a thousand people had signed affidavits and over two thousand still waited in line.

The traffic jams into Lissadown stretched for miles in all directions.

Local businesses started to provide soup and sandwiches free to those standing in line. Pubs and residents allowed people to use their bathrooms. The police tried to persuade people to go home for the night but no one would budge. Instead, they continued to come, a never ending stream of determined citizens who felt let down by the system and who were now going to make a stand. To accommodate the crowds, the police set up extra stations on the cathedral grounds and manned it with volunteers to expedite the process.

Rows and rows of portable toilets were set up in the town center. Extra trains were put on from Cork, Dublin, Galway, Limerick and Belfast. A convoy of ten busloads of students from the university in Cork had become almost one hundred buses and nearly two thousand cars by the time they reached Thurles. The convoy doubled again in number by the time it reached the outskirts of Lissadown.

Brendan Macken's plea for support for Finn

had become a rallying cry for the entire country against injustice and Lissadown was now the epicenter of a people power movement that showed no signs of abatement.

The camera crew walked the line of people waiting, beaming their faces not just to the country but to the whole world as the story of the amazing developments in Ireland began to reach a global audience. The camera showed them all: young, old, rich, poor, standing there together, united in their mission. This was a demonstration unlike anything the country had ever seen.

~ * ~

In Dublin, the Prime Minister convened a meeting with the State Attorney General, Joe Delany's boss. The Prime Minister was in a foul mood. "This situation is getting out of control. It could bring down the whole government if we don't get a handle on it."

The Attorney General nodded. "Yes, sir, I agree."

"You agree? Of course you agree. Only an idiot wouldn't agree. What's your recommendation?" But before the Attorney General could utter a word the Prime Minister continued to rant. "It doesn't seem to me that we can keep this man in jail. Do we even have any evidence against him? My God, I'm wondering why he was arrested in the first place? I swear to you, heads will roll—starting with yours—if I don't get answers soon."

The Attorney General looked around the table at the grim-faced ministers. "It's true that Dr. Lane may have been rather precipitously arrested and that there is as of yet no direct evidence linking him to the crime."

The Prime Minister leapt from his seat, his face red with rage. "Crime? Crime?" he spluttered. "Do you think there is one person in Lissadown right now who thinks a crime has even been committed? In their minds, whoever assaulted those thugs did the town a favor. And from what I've heard, I agree with them. And then there are all of the *witnesses* who swear they were with Dr. Lane? What about them? Are you going to arrest all of them, as Delany has suggested you would?"

"I understand your concerns Prime Minister, and clearly, this is a highly unusual situation. It seems to me, however, that we cannot just drop the charges and release the suspect simply because the people want us to. That would set a dangerous precedent, in my view. I recommend that we continue to hold him and I will look into the matter first thing in the morning. I'll review all the evidence with Delany to make sure the arrest is valid and will report back to you immediately afterwards."

The Prime Minister's tone was deadly calm. "No, you won't. You'll do it tonight. This cannot wait until the morning to get started. Be back here at eight with your recommendation. By the way, I've heard rumors that Delany has links to those crooks. If I find out that's true, I'll see the bastard locked up for the rest of his days."

Chapter Thirty-Seven

Wednesday, August 13, 1986
Week Eight: Day Three

Crowds had continued to flock into Lissadown in droves throughout the night. They were now coming from farther and farther afield as the "Free Finn Lane" movement gathered a head of steam domestically and internationally. The story dominated headlines everywhere and as media coverage expanded exponentially, the pressure on the Irish government to do something increased.

Mike McGill surveyed the throngs of people with growing trepidation. The atmosphere had remained peaceful so far but he knew it wouldn't take much of a spark to convert it into a full scale riot. He had no wish to do battle with people who had simply decided to stand up for their own rights and he was certain none of his men did either. Furthermore, he felt bad for Finn. He had genuinely grown to like him these past few weeks and was very pleased that he and Julia had gotten together.

Nonetheless, given the nature of the attacks, he would have bet his life that Finn had carried them out. McGill wasn't sure how he'd so completely covered his tracks but it was impressive. There wasn't a shred of physical evidence and not only was the Nutt's Haven alibi pure genius, now it was unbreakable.

He had even heard a report that a rally

demanding Finn's release was planned for Saturday in Dublin. Initial estimates were that over four hundred thousand people could attend. He was on tenterhooks, but it was out of his hands.

To his great relief, by ten that morning, the Attorney General released a report indicating that there were grounds to drop the charges against Finn but that further investigations of the attack should be carried out. The report also suggested that possible links had been discovered between Joe Delany and the criminal gang whose leaders had been attacked.

Within minutes, McGill's phone rang.

Less than an hour later, Finn was a free man.

Chapter Thirty-Eight

Monday, August 18, 1986
Week Nine: Day One

Finn had hoped that the modest crowd who had been at Nutt's Tavern that night would confirm his presence there. Two months earlier, when the entire populace of Lissadown was in the gang's grips he couldn't have counted on that. But in that time the tide had begun to turn against the gang. Still a very small part of him worried. That every single person there that night came forward had quieted that fear.

But the editorial published in *The Lissadown Examiner* had touched him. McGill personally brought Finn a copy as soon as he became aware of it. Finn had read it over and over.

Now is the time to look evil in the face and say, "No More."

That had summed it up for him.

However, the outpouring of support from the entire country left him speechless.

It had taken until Monday for things to settle down into something that resembled normal. When Finn sat down at his desk on Monday morning it felt as if he were starting a fresh, new chapter in his life.

Laura hadn't arrived to the office yet. He smiled to himself. She'd been seeing this guy for weeks now. After the first few weeks, she had regained some balance and gotten back into a more normal routine. However, this past weekend the entire town had celebrated. She and her boyfriend must have indulged a bit too freely as well.

Finn realized that he had been so focused on Julia and the gang situation over the last few weeks, he had never asked Laura about this guy. Given everything that had been going on, he figured she'd forgive his poor manners, but he would have to be a little more sociable going forward.

Laura arrived over an hour late, looking completely hung over and wearing clothes that looked, and smelled, as if she had spent the entire weekend in them. He had never seen her like this.

"Jesus Christ al-frigging-mighty. What the hell happened you?"

"I know, I know," Laura replied. "It doesn't look good but I have to get to a meeting or I'll be in trouble."

"Whoa," said Finn, standing up. "No way you can go to that meeting, you'll get sacked. Go home, get a shower and get cleaned up. I'll cover for you. Then you tell me exactly what happened. This I've got to hear."

"Thanks." Laura looked relieved. "I don't think I could honestly sit through a three hour meeting in this condition."

When she returned it was well after noon and Finn had just made himself a cup of tea. "Perfect timing. I'm all ears."

Laura sighed. "I shouldn't be telling you this but I have a feeling you'd pester me forever if I don't. So you know I've been seeing this guy for a while."

"Yup, but you've never told me anything about

him. Who is he? How'd you meet him? What does he do?"

"Jesus, give me a chance to answer one question before firing off a dozen more. You know a bunch of the single Roan employees go out for a pint or two at Nutt's Tavern every Friday."

"I didn't know that."

"Ah, well, I was going to ask you to join us on your first Friday there but you caused a bit of a stir that day and you weren't in any shape to go out. By the next week it looked like you and Julia were an item, so I didn't bother. So anyway, a bunch of us hang out at Nutt's Tavern on Fridays. It's kind of the unofficial 'Roan Pub'."

"I know that, Laura. Can we get back to the story?"

"Right. Well, because it's mostly the Roan guys there, I rarely meet anyone new. But one night—it might have been when you were in Lugano—there was a guy there I'd never seen before, sitting alone at the bar. We were all there, just talking about work and stuff and after a while, he just came right up to me and said, 'You are such a beautiful woman. Could I please buy you a drink?' Now let's face it. Nobody has ever said this to me before so no way was I going to turn him down."

Finn laughed. "Now that was a bold move. Smooooooooth."

"Well, he is American after all. I guess it kind of goes with the territory."

"American? From what part?"

"California, of course." She grinned. "Blond

hair, blue eyes. Your classic surfer dude."

"So what's he doing in Lissadown? Not a blessed wave in sight for miles?"

"He works for Innotech in the US and he's been transferred to their branch over here for six months working on a secret communication cevice that he said he couldn't talk about. So, we had a drink, then another. He was fun to talk. He wanted to know all about me and what I did and everything. Anyway, by the end of the night he asked me out and we've been dating since then."

"So why did you come in so trashed this morning?"

"Everything was so crazy last week with everything that happened and all. And then everyone was celebrating. He doesn't need much of an excuse to party. But Nutt's has been packed all week, so Friday night we went to a nightclub and, well, we kind of got into the spirit of things. We left the club completely trashed and staggered to his apartment and kind of…carried on all weekend."

Finn stared at her in amazement. "You never left his apartment all weekend? What the hell did you do all that time?"

Laura scrunched up her nose. "I think I've said too much already. Promise me you won't tell anyone."

"I promise."

Laura put her face in her hand and a deep red blush rose in her cheeks. "Well if you must know, we drank, we smoked dope and we fucked all weekend. We hardly left the bed at all. There, how's that for a weekend?"

"Wow." Finn whistled. "I'm impressed. He must be quite a stud. I hope you were being careful."

"Yes, well, here's the thing." Laura wrung her hands nervously. "I wasn't careful, and given the time of the month and the number of shots on goal he took, if there's any bit of fertility in either of us, I'm in big trouble."

Finn frowned. "That's not good. Still you had fun, right?"

"Yes, I did. Only…Finn Lane, if I tell you this and you don't keep it to yourself I'll never speak to you again. You can't even tell Julia."

"I promise. Not even Julia."

"Oh God." Laura groaned loudly. "I can't believe I'm actually going to tell you this. He was a bit kinky."

"A bit kinky?"

"Well, more than a bit kinky."

"In what way? You mean sexually?"

"Is there another way to be kinky?" Laura retorted. "Yes, I mean sexually. We were drunk and high and I let him do all kinds of things. At first it was just small stuff, like tying me up."

"You consider being tied up a small thing?"

"In comparison to other thinks, yes."

"What other things?"

"Spanking."

"You let him hit you?"

"Just on the ass. At first it was kind of hot, but he got a little carried away and…uh…he…" She blushed a deeper red. She covered her face with her hands and blurted out, "He went in the back door.

There, I've said it. Judge me now."

Finn just stared at her. "He just...did it? Without asking or anything?"

"Not exactly. Like I said, I was drunk and stoned. I was scared and at first I said no, but it really pissed him off. So I let him. And that's the story of my lost weekend."

"Are you okay?"

"Yeah. Sore and hungover, but okay."

"So now that you've sobered up, are you going to kick what's-his-name to the curb?"

"His name is Cam, and no. I really like him. We just let things get out of hand this weekend. It won't happen again."

"Be sure to tell him if he ever hurts you, I'll kick his ass back to California."

She grinned at him. "And Finn Lane is back on duty."

Chapter Thirty-Nine

October, 1986
Two Months Later

Life had gradually settled into a fairly relaxed routine for both Finn and Julia. The media frenzy continued for a couple of weeks after he was released but eventually it began to fade as other events took precedent. For Finn that couldn't have happened a moment too soon.

Julia moved out of her house and into his. He fell more in love with her every day that passed and he could tell she was equally as happy. Things were definitely looking up. He was enjoying work and he was back to peak fitness, so much so that he began to consider returning to competition. Julia wasn't crazy about this idea but didn't try to put him off either.

"I'm just thinking about it right now," he assured her. "I think I've gone soft. I've been away from it for so long."

Julia just chuckled. "Yeah, right. There are loads of people out there who would beg to differ with you on that score."

One Sunday evening, Finn was relaxing in the kitchen with a cup of tea, reading the newspaper as Bruce Springsteen played softly in the background. He had told Julia about Whitney Campbell and his time in America. Julia had felt such pity for Whitney and remarked that it put her own situation into a very different perspective.

The doorbell rang, disturbing the peace of the evening. Julia had just gotten into the bath.

"Damn it. Who could that be?" Julia had just gotten into the bath, so he set the newspaper aside and answered door.

Mike McGill stood there.

"Uh oh, the last time you made a house call here, Chief Superintendent, it didn't work out that well for me. Should I be worried?"

"I don't know. Should you? Have you done something wrong?"

Finn shook his head with a smile. "Not that I'm aware of."

"Right then, nothing to be worried about so. Now, can I come in or are we going to stand in the doorway all night?"

Finn stepped aside to let McGill in. "I just made tea. Would you like a cup?"

"Tea?" McGill shook his head. "Tea? No, my boyoh, no tea tonight." He produced a bottle from his overcoat pocket. "This here is thirty-year-old Red Breast. The finest whiskey ever distilled. I was given this bottle many years ago and I thought to myself that I'd put it away for a very special occasion and share it with a very special someone. That's tonight and you."

Finn was genuinely taken aback. "Wow, I'm very flattered. What are we celebrating?"

"Well, if you'd get us some glasses, I'll tell you. By the way, where's Julia?"

"In the bath. She just got in about a minute before you got here so it will be at least an hour before she remerges. Ice?"

"Jesus Christ and all the saints, are you soft in the head or what? You can't put ice into this unadulterated nectar. Honestly, young people today. Idiots, the whole lot of them."

He was still muttering when Finn went to get glasses. He was curious about what they were celebrating but he knew McGill well enough now to know that all would be revealed.

"There you go, Chief Superintendent." Finn handed him a glass. "I broke the out the good Waterford for this auspicious occasion. Actually, it's Julia's Waterford so don't drop it or there'll be hell to pay."

McGill poured them each a very healthy measure of whiskey, raised his glass and looked Finn in the eye. "*Sláinte.*"

"*Sláinte,*" Finn repeated as he took a sip. It was indeed excellent. "Very nice. I'm glad you brought it my way. By the way, technically this is your jurisdiction, but are you driving?"

"Well spotted, but no, I'm not. There's a young officer parked by the side of the road who'll wait until I'm ready and who'll drive me home."

"Doesn't he want to come in?"

McGill shook his head. "No, he does not. He's delighted to have the opportunity to drive me, especially when I'm meeting you. For some strange reason, you're a hero to all these guys."

Finn smiled and shrugged.

"Anyways," McGill continued, "we have a few things to celebrate. First, the case against you has been completely and irrevocably dismissed. Done and dusted. I'll drink to that." He raised his glass.

Finn did likewise. He was very relieved. Even though he knew it was unlikely that he would be prosecuted there had always been a risk as long as it was classified as an active investigation. Joe Delany had been totally discredited when his links to Lissadown's criminal gang were unearthed. He was now undergoing investigation himself and it did not look good for him. His replacement had shown no appetite to go after Finn and was not going to take the risk of turning the whole country upside down trying to prosecute whoever had taken down one of the worst criminal gangs in the country.

Finn also knew that Julia would be delighted when she heard this news. She was constantly on edge worrying that Finn could be re-arrested at any moment and potentially locked away for a very long time.

"Another toast. I've finally handed my papers in. I'm retiring. *Sláinte.*" McGill took a deep drink out of his glass.

Finn smiled. "Well, congratulations. *Sláinte.*"

"I think we need another one," McGill opined and refilled their glasses. "It's well past time I was gone anyway. I wanted to retire a few years ago but I was persuaded to stay and try to keep things from getting worse. A piss poor job I did of that. Now, thanks to you—" He raised his glass to Finn. "—I can at least leave with some pride intact and be comforted that those bad days are well behind the town. You've taken the town back. Sad that one single man was able to achieve what a whole police force failed to do."

"I think you're overestimating my role and downplaying your own. Either way, I think you're making the right decision. I'll drink to that. *Sláinte.*"

"I most definitely am making the right decision. Timing couldn't be better. By the way, I went to see Delany."

"Oh yeah?" Finn couldn't keep from laughing. "You went to gloat, right?"

"I did not." McGill looked mildly affronted for a moment before his face split in a broad smile. "Actually, yes, I did. I wanted to look the bastard in the eye and make sure he fully understood that he lost and the good folks won."

"I'm surprised he agreed to see you."

"Hah. He had no frigging say in the matter. I'm still Chief Superintendent and I went there in an official capacity. He's done for. We've found a long trail of financial links between him and those criminals. He'll go away for a long, long time, and he'll serve hard time. There won't be anyone in jail who'll look out for him. Couldn't happen to a nicer guy. I'll drink to that."

"Me too." Finn raised his glass. "*Sláinte.*"

"Here's another reason to celebrate. Sarah and little Jane are coming home from London for good next weekend. They're going to live with us. I was speaking to the little one on the phone last week and she told me that she was so excited that she's going to get her own room all to herself. They only have a single bedroom flat in London so this will be a big change for her. I asked her what color did she want her wall painted and you know what she said to me?"

Finn shook his head, smiling. He knew how much McGill doted on his granddaughter and he could see that he was already getting emotional telling this story.

McGill took another deep slug. "She said, 'Granda, how many walls are in my room?' 'Four, sweetheart,' I told her. She said, 'Four walls? So can I have one red, one blue, one green and one pink?' Her mother took the phone off her and said not to pay attention to her and that I should just pick one color myself and leave it at that. I just asked her to put me back on to my granddaughter because we had important things to discuss and I told her that she absolutely could have her room painted those colors. And you know what? I just finished painting yesterday. She has one red wall, one blue wall, one green wall and one pink wall."

Finn arched a brow at him.

McGill laughed. "It's actually not as bad as it sounds, honestly. If she doesn't like it, I'll paint it again. It's that simple. *Sláinte*."

Finn was beginning to feel the effects of the alcohol now but he was determined to keep pace with McGill, who clearly was an established whiskey drinker.

McGill continued. "Funny thing happened last night. I was passing by Jane's bedroom and I saw the wife standing there just looking around. It's all fully furnished and we got her the 'big girl's bed' that she had asked for. Anyway, I asked the wife if she was all right and she just smiled the biggest smile ever and said that she couldn't wait for them to come home and for us to a be a proper family all over again. Then she said she had something to show me and she hoped I wasn't going to get too angry with her. She led to the closet in the other spare bedroom. It was filled with all sorts of toys, books and games that she had been buying for the past few weeks hoping this day would come. As we stood there, I could see she was kind of worried that I might get upset with her." McGill chuckled. "Instead, I took her by the hand and led her out to the shed where I had stashed all of books, toys and games that I had been buying these past few weeks. We just stood there, held each other and laughed for the longest time. Big, happy laughs. It's been a long time since we felt that good. Magic."

McGill took another drink, sat back in his armchair. "That's enough about me. What are your plans?"

"I'll tell you what his plans are," said Julia as she entered the room. "Hello Chief." She gave McGill a big hug and a kiss. "He's going to settle here in Lissadown, that's what. And," she continued with a mischievous grin on her face, "he's going to ask me to marry him."

Finn stared at Julia, then at McGill then back at Julia. McGill clapped his hands in glee. Before Finn could respond, Julia spoke again. "But he had better do it soon otherwise I won't be able to fit into my dress."

This last statement threw both men for a complete loop for a moment.

Finn jumped to his feet, completely shocked. Could she be?

Julia laughed. "There he goes again. He's doing his fish out of water impression. I've told him before it's not an attractive look."

Finn finally found his voice. "Jules, is it true? Are you really pregnant?"

"Yes dear. I'm really pregnant. I know they thought I might not be able to, after what happened, but I am. Ten weeks. So you'd better get a move on. I'm not waddling down the aisle like a heifer in a white dress."

She turned to McGill who was sitting there grinning like a Cheshire cat. "So Chief, after I say yes to the lucky bastard, I was wondering if you'd do me the honor of giving me away."

McGill appeared completely overwhelmed by this. He got to his feet and with tears streaming down his cheeks he wrapped his arms around Julia. "I'd be absolutely honored, my dear. Absolutely honored." Finally he let go and stepped back, a little unsteadily. "Now, it's time for me to leave. I'm an old man. My heart can't take this much excitement in one evening. Anyway, I'm sure you young folks have lots to talk about. We'll bring you over for dinner, when the kids are settled back and start making wedding plans. I came here to celebrate a special night with Finn, little did I know how big a night it was going to turn into. I'm so happy for you both."

They walked him to the door and when Julia shut it she turned around to Finn. "I hope I didn't spoil—"

She got no further. Finn had dropped to one knee and held an open box with a ring inside it.

"Julia Davis, will you please do me the honor of becoming my wife and spending the rest of your life with me?"

"How…but…how?"

"I've been waiting these past few weeks for the right opportunity to ask you and I think tonight will be hard to beat."

"Yes, oh yes, yes, yes," she said, slipping the ring on her finger. "Thank you so much. It's absolutely gorgeous. I had no idea you had done this. You're very devious."

"I'm glad I kept it as a surprise. But Jules, a baby. I can't believe it. I had fully reconciled myself to the fact that it couldn't happen and I was perfectly fine with that. But this is amazing. When did you find out?"

"I've known for a few weeks but I was so scared to tell you in case something went wrong. I didn't want to get your hopes up. Finally I decided I was going to tell you tonight. I ran the bath but I just sat there on the toilet seat thinking. I'm hoping it's not too soon for us. It turns out that you got me pregnant that very first time. Can you believe that? Now take me to bed."

Chapter Forty

December, 1986
Two Months Later

The past two months had flown by in a whirlwind of frenzied activity and suddenly it was here, their wedding day.

Finn and Julia had scrambled to get everything finished in time. Invitations were printed and sent out. Initially, they thought that they would hold just a simple, quiet ceremony but those thoughts were quickly dashed given the intense media and public interest in their wedding.

Six weeks before the wedding, Julia went shopping with Mike McGill's daughter and wife for a dress. She fretted that by the time the wedding came it wouldn't fit her. She needn't have worried. The dress fit perfectly on her wedding day and there were no visible signs yet that she was pregnant.

They had quickly agreed on their honeymoon. They both loved France so they decided they would just tour around the countryside with no fixed itinerary and stop wherever took their fancy. Finn teased Julia that she was going to be doing a lot of driving since he planned to sample lots of the local wine. For Julia, not being able to drink was a miniscule sacrifice to make and one she was more than happy with.

In spite of the mad scramble, Finn and Julia had remained in remarkably good humor throughout this crazy period. In fact, they had had only one disagreement and it was about Margo Kirk. Finn was adamant that she should not be invited to the wedding but Julia took the opposite view. Finn had asked David to be his best man and he wanted Mrs. Kirk to come also. Julia had reasoned that they couldn't then exclude Margo.

"We can't do that, Finn. It will be a direct slap in the face. Furthermore, Dave and his mom will wonder why. What are we going to say then?"

They had never told David about the incident with Margo and although they had spent a fair amount of time these past six months with David and his fiancé, the subject had never come up.

"She's toxic, Jules. I just don't want her there. I certainly don't want to give her the opportunity of getting a few drinks into her and creating a scene at the reception. You know she is more than capable of doing that."

"Look, let's let bygones be bygones. She tried to destroy us as a couple. It very nearly worked but it didn't. Here we are a few short weeks away from getting married and just months away from having a baby that we thought wasn't even remotely possible. Come on, we're happy and we're lucky. Let's appreciate that and be more forgiving of others."

Finn had reluctantly conceded. "I'm not happy about this, but okay. However, I intend to talk to her about her behavior."

"You do that." Julia kissed him. "You hide it well, but you're a good man."

Now, as Finn stood in the courtyard of the

cathedral in Lissadown amidst the throngs of people, both guests and curious onlookers, not to mention the large numbers of reporters and cameramen, he spotted Margo Kirk heading his way. She was wearing an extremely short, tightfitting red dress that emphasized her long legs and the shapeliness of her figure. She looked stunning and heads turned to look as she passed by.

Finn felt a sense of growing trepidation as she approached though he had to admit that she looked very calm and composed and seemed to be a far different Margo than the one who had nearly destroyed his relationship with Julia.

"Hi Finn. Look, I'm really, really sorry for the trouble I caused you and Julia. That was horrible and I feel so bad. I don't know what came over me. I'm so glad you invited me. I was sure you wouldn't and I would have fully understood if you hadn't."

Finn didn't know what to think. She did appear contrite but then you never knew with Margo. What you thought you saw was seldom what you got. "Hi Margo. Glad you could come. We both wanted you here today."

"Thanks Finn. I'll thank Julia later myself. I want to be sure I get a chance to do so. Look, I know you're probably worried that I'll have a few drinks and create a ruckus at the reception. I swear to you, that won't happen. Put that worry out of your head, please. There won't be any incidents from me at the reception."

She said this with such conviction that Finn almost began to relax. "To tell you the truth, it had crossed my mind, Margo, but I'm glad to hear your reassurance."

"Go enjoy your wedding." She leaned in and hugged him.

Finn thought that it might have been a tad too tight or lasted a beat or two too long but it was so hard to tell that he put it out of his mind.

Finn glanced around the churchyard to see if he could spot Laura and her mysterious boyfriend. He and Julia had tried multiple times over the last few months to get together with Laura and Cam, but it never seemed to work out. Finn was really curious about the guy and wanted to meet him before things got crazy. He finally spotted her but she was alone.

He walked over to her.

"Okay, please tell me he's here and I'm going to get to meet California Cam today."

"Hello to you too. Thanks for the compliment. I know I look very nice."

Finn smiled apologetically. "Sorry. That was very rude of me. You do look beautiful."

"I was only messing with ya. And no, he's not here. At least, not yet. He promised me faithfully that he would be here but he's trying to get something finished at work that's very urgent. He'll be along later. He wouldn't miss it, a real Irish wedding and all. Besides," she gave Finn a sly look, "he's very in to me."

Finn rolled his eyes. "So I hear. Give it a rest. I was hoping to meet him before the ceremony but I'll see you both afterwards. I need to go into the church. The bride will hopefully be here soon."

The church was a peaceful reprieve from the media circus outside. Finn agreed they could take what pictures or videos they wanted outside but the ceremony itself was off limits. There was a bit of grumbling at this but it was clear that Finn was not going to yield so everyone agreed.

Julia had gone to stay at the McGills' last night and would be brought to the church from there with Mike.

Finn and David sat in the front pew and the guests arrived. They reminisced about the old days and planned for the future. The casual conversation kept Finn from getting too nervous. He had to make a note of this, David was getting married in three months and he had asked Finn to be his best man. He might need the same treatment.

Then, only five minutes late, the music started up and everyone turned to the back of the church. Julia had entered arm in arm with Mike McGill and stood there waiting to walk up the aisle to greet her husband to be. Finn was mesmerized. She looked absolutely stunning.

David elbowed him in the side. "Stand up."

Finn continued to just stare down the church at Julia.

David elbowed him again, harder.

Finn turned to him in confusion. "What?"

"Stand up. You have to stand up, you gobshite."

"Oh, yeah." He stood.

David just shook his head. "I'll be like that in a few months myself."

When Julia and Mike reached the top of the church, Finn stepped out of the pew. Mike shook his hand, then grabbed Finn in a bear hug saying,

"You look after her now, you hear."

"I will," Finn promised.

Mike turned to Julia, lifted her veil, kissed her on the cheek and whispered, "You look amazing. I'd marry you myself if I wasn't promised to someone else."

"Cheeky devil," she whispered back. "You clean up well yourself. Who'd have thought that?"

Father Martin, the local parish priest, officiated the ceremony. He had gotten to know Julia in the past year and a half and was aware of how much she had suffered. He seemed delighted that things had worked out for her.

When it was Julia's turn to take her vows, she reached out and took Finn's face in her hands, looked into his eyes and after she said the words "'til death do us part" she added in a whisper, "I don't ever want to be without you."

Vows exchanged, they sat back and waited for Father Martin to give a sermon. Instead he said, "I know it's a bit unusual but the bride has requested that she'd like to sing a song."

Finn looked at Julia in surprise. They had discussed the ceremony in detail and this had never come up.

She whispered, "This is for you," then she walked to the lectern. She removed the microphone and went to the center, in front of the altar. She stood for a moment looking out at the expectant crowd in the jam packed church, then lifted the microphone.

"The song I'm about to sing is very special to me. I love both the melody and the message. During the deepest, darkest moments of my life, I'd play this song as reminder that there is always light at the end of the tunnel, there is always hope and if you truly believe that you can make it, you will. Now, I want to sing it for you all, but particularly for Finn, the beautiful, strong, loving man who brought me and an entire community back into the light. I am blessed to have him as a husband and the father of the little life within me."

Then, in a very clear, beautiful voice, she began to sing, *The Rose*. When she got to the last verse, she turned and looked directly at Finn as she began to sing those final uplifting words that so mirrored her own life.

Finn loved her so very much he thought his heart would burst. He was so mesmerized by her, he scarcely registered the sound of footsteps that broke the silence. But then Julia's brow furrowed momentarily, then her puzzled look changed rapidly to sheer terror. He turned his head to see what had spooked Julia so. An instant later he was out of his seat and dashing towards her. He dove at her and tried to envelope her in his arms just as the shots began to ring out. He lay on top of Julia as the noise in the church turned from gasps of shock to sheer panic.

Someone screamed, "Get the gun, get the gun."

Then another shot rang out, loud and harsh over the spreading pandemonium followed seconds later by yet another shot. Slowly and carefully, he lifted himself off Julia for a second only to see red blood stains start to spread out wider and wider on Julia's white dress.

His world shattered.

~ * ~

That evening, as the story made headlines all over the world, the most memorable image was an iconic picture captured by a photographer who'd entered the church at the sound of gun fire.

In the tragic scene, Finn knelt on the altar, cradling his bride, blood blossoming across her gown. David knelt in the aisle, his dead sister in his arms. Both of them wore expressions of such abject sorrow, it was impossible not to be moved.

It was the photograph of a lifetime that captured pain and sorrow in their rawest and most visceral elemental states. The picture, published in hundreds of newspapers and magazines, would eventually be on the cover of Time Magazine and was ultimately awarded the prize of Photo of the Year.

Finn learned later that Margo Kirk, the girl he hadn't wanted to invite to the wedding, was the one who had screamed, "Get the gun," as she had rushed out of her seat and attempted to reach the shooter. She had been killed instantly by a bullet to her heart. The assailant had then turned the gun on himself, firing a bullet into his mouth.

In the split second Finn had spared to glance down the aisle as he rushed to try and save Julia, he knew instantly who the man with the gun was.

Morgan Herman.

Chapter Forty-One

It had been nerve-rackingly touch and go for a harrowing forty-eight hours but incredibly, both Julia and the baby she was carrying survived. Finn's lightning quick reflexes, coupled with the fact that Morgan had used an old manual revolver, had given him a split second chance to save them. As a result, just one of the three bullets Morgan had fired hit Julia and mercifully it was far enough away from the baby that no permanent damage had been done when the bullet was removed during the very delicate and intricate operation.

Morgan Herman, who had died instantly in the church after firing a bullet into his mouth, had done so not knowing he'd failed in his mission.

In the first hours, as Finn paced the surgical waiting room with Mike McGill, he could not fathom how Morgan Herman could have been in the church. Eventually, Mike was able to make a few calls and they learned that Morgan was none other than Cam White, Laura's boyfriend.

"Cam White. Cam White. It's a play on Whitney Campbell. Damn it, why didn't I put that together? Margo's dead and Julia is fighting for her life because of my stupidity."

"Christ almighty, Finn, stop torturing yourself. Who would have made that connection?"

When she was finally out of surgery, Finn had stayed by Julia's side in the hospital the whole time, refusing to eat and unable to sleep. He just sat there holding her hand as she clung to life. He talked to both her and their unborn child, urging them both to pull through no matter what.

Whether this had made a difference or not, something worked as gradually the doctors became more optimistic about their chances of survival. Finally after two days of desperation, they declared them both out of danger. Finn almost collapsed with relief and allowed himself reluctantly to be led away from her bedside by Mike McGill so that the doctors could continue to care for her. He refused to go far and McGill had to practically force feed Finn some sandwiches, standing in the corridor immediately outside Julia's room.

McGill had ensured that officers were posted outside the hospital entrance and the entrance to the ward where Julia was. The media and public interest in Julia's status was as global as it was intense. It seemed that the whole country had waited with bated breath for every single update.

Vigils sprang up in all corners of the country as people gathered to pray in silence for Julia's survival. Somber candlelight processions were held in numerous towns and cities and the empathy and good will that ordinary people showed towards Julia was beyond touching. Perhaps the largest gathering though, was the one outside of the hospital. There were people there, night and day, praying for her and hoping she'd pull through.

When the good news broke, the crowd erupted in cheers and tears which echoed across the country. Even the hard-nosed police officers who were stationed at the hospital could be seen with tears of joy and relief in their eyes.

An elderly woman who had been among those keeping vigil at the hospital was interviewed by a television reporter. She said, "There was too much love for her and her baby in this country. God was never going to let her die."

And Finn had to agree.

~ * ~

Finn was sitting by the bed when Julia finally opened

her eyes. She looked at him and whispered, "The baby?"

Finn's face broke into a huge smile as he choked back his tears. "He's fine, and so are you."

Julia closed her eyes again and breathed a huge sigh of relief as she too broke into tears. She lay there for a moment in silence, sobbing softly, then opened her eyes again. "So it's a boy, huh? How do you know?"

Finn laughed. "I'm highly confident of it."

Julia smiled, waited a moment and whispered, "It could be a girl, you know."

Finn just beamed back at her. "I'm highly confident of that too."

"Idiot." It thrilled him to see a hint of a twinkle in her eye.

"You must be feeling better, if you're already giving me hell."

Julia closed her eyes again and remained silent for so long that Finn thought she had fallen back asleep.

"You were here the whole time, weren't you?"

"I was. I didn't have anywhere better to go."

"It's weird. I know I was out of it, but I felt like I could sense your presence and hear your voice. It kind of made me want to keep fighting and not let go. Besides, you need me here to keep you in line."

"You have no idea how much I'm looking forward to that."

Julia closed her eyes for a few more minutes. When she opened them again, her expression was somber. "What happened? Who was that crazy guy with the gun? Was he a gang member?"

Finn thought for a moment. Maybe it would be better to let her believe that for the time being, he thought. There'd be plenty time for her to learn the truth when she was stronger. But he'd kept the truth from her once before and it nearly destroyed them. Plus, if she thought the gang was after them, it might terrify her.

"Finn, what happened?"

"Do you remember me telling you about Whitney Campbell and Morgan Herman?"

She frowned. "Yes."

"Well, the shooter was Morgan Herman."

"How...why?"

"The how is pretty clear. Of course he knew I was a student at Cork University. Apparently, he came to Ireland looking for me, just after I came to Roan. He was a smart guy. He apparently made a few friends, asked a few questions and found out where I'd gone."

"So he found out you were here. How did he get into the wedding?"

"He came to Lissadown and did the same thing. It's a small enough town. He hung out in different pubs until he figured out where most of the Roan employees went. He was biding his time, looking for a way in to hit the jackpot."

"What do you mean?"

"He chatted up Laura at Nutt's Tavern one night. Somewhere along the way, he figured out that she was my office mate."

"He was the mysterious boyfriend?"

Finn nodded grimly. "We invited him to the wedding."

"But why did he want to kill me?"

"That's a tougher question. Once I knew it was him, McGill liaised with cops in the States to see if the story could be pieced together. As best they could tell, Morgan's family knew he had some mental issues for which he was medicated. When Whitney was found murdered, they moved heaven and earth looking for him. They found him in Canada. He'd gone off his meds. They got him straightened out and moved him to England. On his meds again, he seemed to settle in to a quiet life. Not wanting him to risk being recognized, they encouraged him to bleach his hair blond, grow a mustache and wear bright blue contacts."

"And they just left him on his own after he'd murdered someone?"

Finn shook his head. "I guess no one wants to see the worst in their children. His parents believed he was not a danger. But apparently, before they got him back on his meds, he had raged on and on about me. In his twisted brain he had convinced himself that the *voice* he heard, telling him to kill Whitney, was mine. Since, in his mind, I took his love away, he wanted to take someone from me."

Julia frowned. "I'm sure Laura's shattered."

"She is. She blames herself. But there is absolutely no way she could have known he was anything but what he said he was. Morgan is clever and personable."

"So exactly what happened? Was anyone else hurt?"

Finn really didn't want to tell her this but it couldn't be avoided. "Morgan had an old manual revolver. He fired the first bullet and it hit you. The person closest to him was Margo." Finn took a deep breath. He was very cut up over Margo's death. "She jumped in front of him. I think she was trying to get the gun. She took the next two bullets."

"Oh, dear God. Is she okay?"

"She was killed instantly. Then Morgan killed himself."

Julia closed her eyes and tears slipped down her cheeks. Finn held her hand tightly. After a minute, she opened her eyes. "How's David?"

"Devastated. God, Julia, I'm so sorry. This is all my fault."

"How the hell did you arrive there?"

"Morgan came here because of me."

"Morgan came here because he was ill."

Finn shook his head and looked away.

"Finn, look at me."

He dragged his eyes back to hers.

"You are a smart, strong, wonderful man. But no

matter how smart, strong and wonderful you are, you are just one man. This was all outside of your control. Don't start our married life weighed down by misplaced guilt. Please. Promise me."

He sighed and let her words of absolution wash over him. She was right. They had to go forward. He leaned down and kissed her gently. "I promise."

Julia closed her eyes, appearing to doze for a few minutes. "What day is it?"

"Tuesday."

"We were supposed to fly to France tonight. We aren't going to have our honeymoon."

Finn cleared his throat. "Yeah, well, about that. I thought it would be a shame to waste the tickets so I figured I'd just go on by myself tonight. You don't mind, do you?"

"Finn Lane. If I had the energy, I'd smack you."

"You could, but I'm pretty good at taking a punch."

"That's what I hear."

"So, since it's a 'no' on me going to France alone, I have another idea. After the baby is born, we'll christen him Francis and then the three of us will go to France and have that honeymoon. It will be different to what we planned but I think it might be even more special."

Just then a nurse entered the room to shoo Finn away so Julia could get some rest.

Finn reluctantly agreed. He stood up and kissed Julia softly. "I'll be right outside."

As he reached the door, Julia called, "Hey Finn, what if it's a girl?"

"No problem. We'll call her Francesca and still go on the trip."

He smiled at the sound of her soft laughter.

~ * ~

Four days after that, Margo Kirk was quietly laid to rest in a little cemetery in West Cork. Finn attended alone as Julia was still in hospital. He was almost glad of that as he didn't want her to have to suffer through what turned out to be a painfully emotional day.

After saying tearful goodbyes to David and Mrs. Kirk, Finn got back on the road that evening to drive to Lissadown. He found it hard to concentrate with the volume of thoughts flowing through his mind.

Whitney, Brian Davis, and Margo, all dead now.

He thought of Morgan Herman and how messed up he'd been. He too was dead.

"Too many deaths. So unnecessary."

He thought about Julia and their baby and a smile worked its way onto his face for the very first time that day.

"Hold that thought," he told himself. "The sun is starting to melt the snow."

About The Author

Ford Murphy was born and raised in Ireland and moved to the US with his wife in the mid-1990's. Since then, they have lived in the greater Washington DC area, where they are raising their three children. Taking The Town is the author's debut novel. A second book, also featuring Finn Lane, is currently in progress. Ford Murphy is a pseudonym honoring the author's grandmothers.

Other Titles by Duncurra LLC

New York Times Bestselling Author Kathryn Lynn Davis

Highland Awakening

Sing to Me of Dreams

Coming in January 2017, the long awaited sequel, Weave for Me a Dream.

Award Winning, Best-Selling Author Lily Baldwin

The Scottish Outlaw Series

Jack: A Scottish Outlaw

Quinn: A Scottish Outlaw

Rory: A Scottish Outlaw

Award Winning, Bestselling Author Ceci Giltenan

The Pocket Watch Chronicles:

The Pocket Watch

The Midwife

Once Found

The Christmas Present

Coming in January 2016, The Choice

The Fated Hearts Series

Highland Revenge

Highland Echoes

Highland Angels

The Duncurra Series

Highland Solution

Highland Courage

Highland Intrigue

Stephanie Joyce Cole

Compass North

MJ Platt

Somewhere Montana

Look for exciting new titles from Duncurra in 2017!

Made in the USA
Middletown, DE
26 January 2017